## THE DEADLY HUNT

Rourke swung the CAR-15 off his shoulder where it had hung muzzle down. He pulled the rubber plug from the muzzle and dropped it into his musette bag where he carried some of his spare magazines and other gear. He shifted the rifle forward, working the bolt and chambering the top cartridge out of the freshly loaded thirty-round stick.

He started forward across the sand, feeling he was being watched, waiting for it to come—

It came.

"Kill him!"

The shout—somehow oddly not quite human.

Rourke wheeled, snapping the CAR-15's muzzle forward, ramming the flash deflector into the face of the man—man?—coming for him. The machete dropped from the right hand as the body reeled.

He turned, hearing something—feeling something. Two men—like the first, half in the clothing of "civilized" men and half in animal skins, unshaven, hair blowing wildly in the wind. One had a long bladed knife secured, lashed to a pole—a primitive pike or spear. The second held a pistol. . . .

# THE SURVIVALIST SERIES
## by Jerry Ahern

**THE SURVIVALIST**

# #6
# THE SAVAGE HORDE

## BY JERRY AHERN

**ZEBRA BOOKS**
**KENSINGTON PUBLISHING CORP.**

ZEBRA BOOKS

are published by

KENSINGTON PUBLISHING CORP.
475 Park Avenue South
New York, N.Y. 10016

Fifth printing: August 1986

Printed in the United States of America

For Fran Hood—friend and stalwart of the entire
Ahern Family—all the best . . .

# Chapter 1

John Rourke pulled up the zipper on the fly of his Levis with his right hand, his left moving across his body plane to the Detonics stainless under his right armpit in the double Alessi rig, his fingers knotting around the black checkered rubber Pachmayr grips, his left thumb poised to cock the .45 as soon as it cleared the leather. He gave the pistol a short, firm tug, hearing the speed break through the trigger guard unsnap. His thumb jerked back the hammer.

Rourke wheeled, the .45 in his left hand snaking out from inside the brown leather bomber jacket, moving forward, his right hand reaching for the gun's twin under his left arm. He already had the target—a man about six-foot four, unshaven, his black leather jacket mud-stained, a riot shotgun in his hands, the pump tromboning as the twelve-gauge, roughly .70 caliber muzzle swung on line. Rourke's trigger finger twitched once, the second Detonics already out, in his right fist, the hammer jacking back. Rourke fired the second pistol as well, the discharge like an echo of the first punctuating the riot shotgun as it fired.

Rourke threw himself down and right, the shotgunner right handed and the impact of Rourke's first slug pounding the man in the right side of the chest, twisting the body right, pulling the shot column right as well. The ground three feet from Rourke seemed to erupt, the .30

caliber-sized pellets raising a spray of loose dirt and dead leaves, the dirt showering down as the shotgunner spun, twisted and lurched toward the lank Georgia pine beside which he'd stood. The body slipped along the length of the pine's trunk, then stopped, almost sagged down to the knees, the shotgun falling as the hands went limp.

Rourke pushed himself to his feet, muttering, "Can't even urinate without somebody tryin' to kill ya—hell." His pistols held close to his sides at hip level, Rourke moved toward the man, Rourke's eyes behind the dark-lensed aviator-style sunglasses scanning from side to side. Where there was one brigand there were usually a dozen or more nearby.

But he saw no one else.

He stopped beside the body—the front of the leather jacket the dead man wore was caught up on a stump of branch. Blood oozed from the right center of the chest over the lung and from the left side of the neck near the hinge of the jaw, the eyes wide open in death, still clear.

Rourke shoved the body down to the ground, letting it flop into the rotted leaves and the brown and brittle pine needles there. The shotgun was a cheapie—Rourke had no interest in it. Rourke unzipped his bomber jacket, shoving one of his Detonics pistols into his belt, the safety upped. His left hand free now, the right fist clenched tight on the other Detonics, Rourke began—methodically—to search the dead man.

A poor-quality lockblade folding knife—Rourke didn't need it. A disposable cigarette lighter—Rourke tried it under his thumb and it lit. He had no use for disposable anythings, but extra fire was always useful—Rourke pocketed the lighter. Cigarettes—Rourke didn't smoke them and he stuffed them back in the dead man's pocket. A Freedom Arms .22 Magnum Boot Pistol. "Hmm," Rourke murmured. He inspected the little gun; it seemed in perfect working order. He searched the pockets, finding a plastic box of fifty rounds, only four holes in the plastic grid for the missing rounds. He stuffed the box of ammo in his bomber jacket patch pocket and put the boot pistol's hammer to half cock, twisted the cylinder base pin and withdrew it, then removed the cylinder. Four rounds, all unfired. He had used the little Freedom Arms guns a few times as last ditch back up ordnance. They worked well and were accurate, despite their size. But he carried no single action revolver ever with a round under the hammer. He pushed out one of the four loaded rounds, using the base pin to urge it out of the charging hole in the cylinder, then reassembled the gun, pocketing the loose fourth round. Rourke tucked the three-inch tubed gun in another pocket, then quickly resumed the search. A wallet; inside it a Pennsylvania driver's license— expired—and the folded up picture of a naked blonde-haired woman. It looked clipped from a magazine, and there was twenty dollars. The money was really useless, more suitable for fire starting than a means of exchange since the Night of The War. Rourke took the twenty and pocketed it anyway, then thumbed closed the eyes.

Looking around the wooded area past the body, he upped the safety on the second Detonics, dropped the pistol in his hip pocket and picked up the shotgun, mechanically emptying the magazine tube. He unscrewed the nut at its front, tossing the nut into the trees, then pulling the magazine spring. He bent and twisted this, then threw it away, letting the emptied and nearly useless smooth bore fall to the ground. It could be fired awkwardly single shot, but there was no time to remove any less obvious parts.

He started back across the clearing now and away from the dead man. More brigands would be coming soon, having heard the gunfire. He was mildly surprised none had come yet. To have left an operable weapon behind him for someone else perhaps to use against him would

9

have been foolish.

As he started to mount the Harley, he thought better of it, turned and pulled down the zipper of his fly, finishing what he'd started to do before the interruption . . .

"I tell ya those was shots—shots. Marty—maybe he's in trouble or somethin', Crip!" His hands shook as he lit a cigarette, the lighter not working for him.

The taller, thinner man crouched beside him in the pines took a Zippo from his pocket and worked it. "Here—and if Marty's in trouble, then that's too fuckin' bad, Jed—too fuckin' bad."

The first man, Jed, poked the tip of the cigarette into the lighter's flame, nodding through a mouthful of smoke, coughing as he said, "But if he bumped into somebody—maybe—"

"Somebody comes this way lookin' for us, we take care a them too—there's plenty of us and only six of them Army guys comin' and if we could hardly hear them shots, a cinch them Army guys didn't." Jed's eyes followed Crip as the taller man turned and glanced down along the defile and toward the valley below. Spotted behind rocks and boulders and trees were more than two dozen men—armed with everything from riot shotguns to automatic weapons. And past these, at the far side of the valley, more visible from the wake of trodden down grass and wild oats tracking their line of march, were six figures in olive drab.

Crip was peering through binoculars now. "Those guys gotta have maybe a coupla hundred rounds of ammo apiece on 'em—and the six M-16s. Maybe got other shit we can use."

"We could use gas better," Jed murmured.

"Yeah—well—with more ammo and better guns, maybe we can get us some gas, too. I been plannin'—"

10

"But killin' Army guys—maybe they're fightin' the Commies or somethin'—maybe—"

"Maybe shit," Crip laughed. "You wanna go fight Commies, go on and do it. Me—I wanna stay alive, stay cookin'—like the guys down there want. I take 'em to war with the fuckin' Russians and they'd run like hell. I take 'em to war to get some neat shit, to have some fun—they stick, they fight. Them Army guys down there's like ever'body else—fair game. They'd plug us soon as shit—but we'll ice 'em first."

Crip went back to looking through the binoculars. Jed puffed anxiously on the cigarette—and his hands still shook . . .

Natalia Anastasia Tiemerovna brushed the dark lock of hair back from her face, dismounting the bike, walking across the clearing. The fingers of her left hand swept back through the hair again, tiny knots in it from riding the bike against the wind. She made a mental note to put her hair up after she brushed it, either that or tie a scarf over it. The fingers of her right hand were half hidden under the full flap of the black leather holster on her right hip, the fingers—all but the first finger—wrapped around the smooth finger-grooved Goncala Alves stocks of the round butted Smith L-Frame, the first finger poised and slightly outstretched, to reach into the revolver's trigger guard as soon as she cleared leather.

She heard a rustling in the trees, but didn't react to it and draw the .357—it was Paul, her eyes having caught sight of his movement in the instant prior to the snapping of the twig. What Paul Rubenstein still lacked in expertise, she felt he more than compensated for by ingenuity and tenacity—and she liked him anyway. She saw a form on the ground at the edge of the trees—but it was unmoving.

Her left hand unsnapped the flap of the Safariland holster on her other hip, both of the customized, slab-side barreled stainless L-Frames coming into her hands and their muzzles leveling toward the treeline's edge. She kept walking, lengthening her stride, glancing down once at her black booted feet beneath the black whipcord slacks.

The leaves—multi-colored the way autumn had always been near Moscow when a little girl on her way to ballet—were beautiful.

She stopped, five yards from the form of the man on the ground—dead. She glanced from side to side, then walked forward, knowing Paul was still in the tree cover, watching for signs of a trap.

Natalia stopped beside the body, kicking it fast once in the exposed rib cage just to be sure, then stepping back quickly. There was no betraying movement—however slight. She holstered the revolver in her left hand, then dropped to her knees.

Her skin touched its skin—still warm. The eyes were closed—unnaturally, by whoever had put the twin holes in the body, she deduced. "Not heartless," she murmured to herself, then more closely inspected the wound in the neck and in the chest. "But very good."

She stood up, walking in the direction from which she judged the shots to have been fired. She stooped to the ground—a piece of brass, still shiny and bright, freshly fired. .45 ACP—Natalia  glanced at the headstamp, recognizing the ammo brand. It was what Rourke carried, as did she herself. "Hmm," she murmured.

There was a second cartridge case and she picked it up, noticing a disturbance in the leaves a few feet further on. She walked toward that, already noting the imprint of motorcycle tracks.

"John?" She studied the tracks. For the last seven days, she and Paul Rubenstein had been searching for him. There was the urgent message from her uncle. There was the fear that somehow Rourke had not survived the storms which had swept the coast and central section of the country. There was the loneliness she felt—and the confusion of purpose, identity. She was Russian—she was helping Americans. America and Russia were technically still at war, despite the fact Soviet forces occupied much of the land. She was KGB—a major.

She shook her head to clear it.

There would be time later to wrestle with herself—wrestle with herself as she had done already.

Natalia walked past the motorcycle tracks, seeing something glistening on the leaves. She bent over, taking a dry leaf and touching it to the moist leaves that had shown the glistening effect. Without bringing it too close to her nose, the smell confirmed her initial suspicion—urine. Probably human. There was another, similar wet spot a few feet to the left.

"Natalia!"

"She glanced behind her. Paul was running toward her, his Schmeisser submachinegun dangling from its sling under his right arm, a riot shotgun—or at least the major pieces of it—in his right hand.

"I found this—somebody deliberately made it inoperable."

"It could still function single-shot—hand chambering. I noticed it, too. I think John was here, Paul—and just a few minutes ago."

"That louder shot was from this—"

"And the two lighter ones from these that we heard," she nodded, showing him the spent cartridge cases.

Rubenstein took them from her, inspecting them. "That's John's brand all right—"

"But also one of the largest ammunition manufacturers in the world—the cases could have been from a thousand other people—ten thousand. But I found this," and she gestured toward the motorcycle tracks. "And signs of someone urinating here about the time we heard the shots. That dead man's flesh is still warm. I think it was John—stopped to—to—"

"To piss," Paul nodded, smiling embarrassedly.

Natalia felt herself smile. "Yes," she nodded. "And somebody came up on him—that man over there. John shot him, then disassembled the shotgun so no one could use it afterward. Then he finished—pissing. Then he drove off."

"But when there's one brigand, there's usually a bunch of 'em—"

"There aren't any signs of them—did you find any?"

"Nothing—no," and Rubenstein shook his head, his left hand pushing his wire-rimmed glasses up off the bridge of his nose, then sweeping across his high forehead through his thinning dark hair.

"And neither did I—if you were John—"

Rubenstein laughed. "Ha—if I were John—if anybody is closer to John in the way they think—you are. What would you do—kill one brigand and figure there are more around?"

"John urinated twice—as if he'd been doing it when he heard the man, then there was the gunfight, then John checked the man's pockets—I noticed that when I checked the body. Then John finished what he'd been doing."

"That's John for you," Rubenstein smiled.

"He would have been here long enough to tell if others were coming—and none did. Which would mean this dead man could have been a straggler—"

"There wasn't any bike—no signs of a truck or anything—"

"Or he could have been alone and on foot."

Paul shook his head. "I don't think so."

"Neither do I—his boots were marked from riding a bike, and the soles were polished almost smooth—but they weren't worn down as if he'd walked a great deal."

"John would have figured there were brigands in the area and whatever they were doing, hearing what maybe would have been gunshots wasn't important enough to pull them away—"

Natalia nodded. "Laying a trap—ambuscade—"

"What?" Rubenstein asked, his face quizzical looking to her.

She felt herself laugh—"That's only English, Paul—ambuscade—it means ambush."

"Ohh," and he nodded. "Yeah—I knew that," and Rubenstein laughed.

She touched her left hand gently to his right forearm. "John is probably looking for the other brigands—the rest of the dead man's gang."

"Can't be more than a couple miles—guy wouldn't have left his wheels—"

"He could have been a scout—maybe from a base camp. But you're right, Paul—not more than a few miles."

"If we can backtrack him through the woods—"

"We'll know soon enough if John did the same thing," she interrupted. "And we can find him—"

"Before he runs into a dozen or two brigands I hope," Rubenstein added soberly.

"Before—yes—come on," and she started running back toward her bike, glancing over her shoulder as Rubenstein threw the useless shotgun into the trees, then started running in the opposite direction—for his bike, she knew.

She reached her own machine, the Harley-Davidson Low Rider Rourke had used in the trek across the West Texas desert, the machine he'd taken from the brigands after they had murdered the survivors of the airliner crash. Paul had told her about it.

"How long ago?" she murmured, thinking of the times they had spent—times of danger, death—but in a strange way, happier times than she had ever known.

She snapped closed the flaps of the Safariland Holsters for the stainless Smith & Wessons on her hips, then straddled the machine.

She brought the engine to life . . .


John Thomas Rourke studied the panorama before him, focusing the armored Bushnell 8x30s on the group of six men moving through the field which covered the valley floor. Camouflage fatigues, crusher hats, M-16s—either Marines or Army—but forces of U.S. II. Likely an intelligence patrol, he surmised.

He swept the binoculars back, along the defile—poorly concealed men and a few women perhaps—though the long hair and distance made it difficult for him to tell. He counted twenty-five brigands at least, and two more further up by the tree line.

Evading a medium-sized brigand band working the territory would be time consuming, time he could utilize in making headway to the Retreat to resupply and link with Paul, time he could use searching for his wife and son and daughter.

He glanced back through the tubes at the six military personnel. They moved too openly, as if inviting attack. That thought had crossed Rourke's mind when first spotting them, but there were no indications there was any large military force operating in the area, using these six as bait. Rourke had to assume ignorance the sole motivation of the six men—or possibly just the ignorance of their commander.

He put down the glasses.

He had replaced the spent cartridges in the twin stainless Detonics pistols, still had ample ammunition for the CAR-15—several loaded magazines full. The Metalified Python, of course.

He pushed himself to his feet—he would leave the jet

black Harley he rode hidden as it already was, then cross behind the ambushers. He looked back once, judging the distance between the six troopers and the waiting brigands.

Two hundred yards—he would have to hurry.

He swung the CAR-15 forward, his right fist locking on the pistol grip, his left hand earing back the bolt, letting it fly forward and chamber the first round from the magazine. His right thumb found the safety, working it on—he was already running.

# Chapter 2

Rourke edged along the rise through the tree line. The two brigands who sat above the rest in the shelter of a pile of rocks were within fifty yards of him now. There were two alternatives—attempting to take out the brigands one at a time through stealth, or sniper fire. The first possibility—because of the sheer weight of numbers and the immediacy of the brigands' opening fire on the six military personnel moving through the valley—was something he decided to rule out.

Rourke shrugged, flattening himself in a solid prone position along the tree line with an outcropping of rocks affording cover against returning fire. He telescoped the CAR-15's stock, settling the metal buttplate against his right shoulder in the pocket, the Colt scope's reticle settling, too—on the spinal column of the nearest brigand. One of the two men in the higher rocks had to be the leader.

His thumb worked the safety to off, the first finger of his right hand touching the trigger.

"Good-bye," Rourke muttered, then began the squeeze, the rifle recoiling against his shoulder, its sharp crack loud in the otherwise still countryside.

He rode it out, the .223's recoil mild enough, the scope showing his work—the brigand holding the binoculars to his eyes slammed forward, up and over the rocks behind which he had hidden himself, the body rolling downward.

The man who had been beside the first man turned around, his mouth opened as if to scream. Rourke shot him in the neck, the body toppling back across the rocks and staying there, the arms flapping up once, then still.

Rourke tucked down, gunfire slamming into the rocks near his position, bullets biting into the tree trunks, bits of bark spraying him as did chips of rock. He pulled back. And there was gunfire now from the six men on the valley floor.

Rourke pushed himself up, the rifle swinging onto targets of opportunity among the brigand band. Two round semi-automatic bursts—one man down. Another target—male or female. Rourke wasn't sure.

There was more answering fire, automatic weapons chewing whole pine boughs from the trees surrounding him, pine needles showering him. Rourke pulled back.

Moving along on knees and elbows, he drew away from the rise, then pushed himself up into a low, running crouch, starting through the tree line. He stopped, rising to his full height beside a greater in diameter than normal pine, shouldering the CAR-15, firing another two round burst. A brigand with what looked like an M-16 was running up the hill toward him, the brigand's body lurching backward, doubling up like a jackknife, then seeming to hesitate in mid-air for an instant, then going down.

Rourke ran on, diving to cover in more of the low rocks as heavy automatic weapons fire tore into the trees.

He pushed up, snapping off a fast two-round burst with the CAR-15, missing, then another two-round burst—a man with a shotgun, one of three men racing up the hill. This time Rourke didn't miss.

He shot a quick glance into the valley—there was fire still coming from the six military personnel in the valley, but seemingly having little effect.

Rourke pushed himself to his feet, backing off into the

trees, spraying a succession of two-round bursts from the hip toward the advancing brigand fire team, nailing one more of them and dropping him, the third man going to cover, but spraying automatic weapon fire into the trees. The tree trunk nearest Rourke erupted with the impact, huge chunks of bark and slivers of green wood pelting at Rourke's face.

Rourke buttoned out the nearly spent thirty-round magazine, ramming a fresh magazine from his musette bag into the well, then firing two more two-round bursts.

He started running laterally again, along the tree line, to give the brigands a moving target, to give the six men in the valley time to close up toward the base of the hill. Fire and maneuver—he hoped as he ran that they were thinking the same thing.

# Chapter 3

Paul Rubenstein slowed his bike, Natalia slowing hers beside him.

"Must be John," he murmured, working open the bolt of the Schmeisser and giving the Browning High Power a good luck tug in the ballistic nylon tanker style shoulder holster across his chest.

Natalia said nothing—Paul watched as she eared back the bolt of her M-16, the rifle slung cross body, diagonally under her right arm, as Rourke carried his.

"Let's go—"

"We can split when we reach the battle site—you take the right flank, I'll take the left," she answered.

"You got it," and Rubenstein revved his machine, punching out, steering the fork wildly as he dodged tree trunks, feeling the bouncing as he jumped hummocks, his cowboy-booted feet balancing him as he reached a shallow defile, the bike jumping over a ridge of earth and coming down, dust flying up around him.

The gunfire was louder now, heavy automatic weapons fire like he'd heard so many times before in the weeks since he'd known John Rourke, in the weeks since the Night of The War. The ground evened out, Rubenstein wrestling the Harley hard right, almost losing it, his left foot dragging the ground as he twisted with his hands, his forearms aching as he pulled the machine upright. He bent low now, building RPMs as he sped the machine along the crest of the rise. There was a forested area a hundred yards ahead, the gunfire coming from just beyond it, heavier even than it had been.

"I'll head through the trees—you go around 'em, Natalia!" Paul shouted.

"Yes, Paul!" he heard her call back, not looking. The idea amused him for an instant—Natalia, the KGB major, the tough fighter, the martial arts expert, the female counterpart of Rourke in almost every skill—"yes, Paul." He laughed at himself.

He was closing the distance into the trees now, jumping the bike over a small hillock of dirt and gravel-sized rock, dodging the fork hard left to miss a tree trunk. It was a deer path he was on—Rourke had described them, shown them to him. He bent lower over the machine, thorns and pine boughs swatting at his face and exposed hands, slapping against his olive drab field jacket. He saw movement in the trees to his far left—it wasn't Natalia on her bike. It was a man, running, firing an assault rifle.

Rubenstein slowed the bike, the rear tire spraying dirt and pine needles, the bike sliding as Rubenstein balanced it out, letting it drop then, running from the bike and into the trees.

The man in the woods was turning around, throwing the assault rifle to his shoulder to fire.

Rubenstein swung the Schmeisser forward on its sling. He wouldn't beat the first burst. He knew that.

Then suddenly, Rubenstein stopped the upward movement of the German MP-40 subgun's muzzle.

It was John Rourke—the tall, dark-haired, lean-faced man with the assault rifle.

Paul Rubenstein couldn't help himself—he let out a yell.

# Chapter 4

The counterfeit rebel yell—with a New York accent. Rourke felt his face seaming with a smile.

"Paul—over here—keep down!"

Rourke wheeled, ducking down himself, a fusillade of automatic weapons fire pouring toward him, hammering into the trees surrounding him. He pumped the CAR-15's trigger, edging back into the trees. He saw a flicker of movement at the base of the hill, along the near edge of the valley. Dark hair blew back straight from the neck, dark clothes—an M-16 firing.

"Natalia!" Rourke shouted the name, astounding himself that he had. Gunfire was pouring toward her on the bike now, the bike wheeling hard right toward the base of the hill, then skidding in the dirt, the woman almost leaping from the machine to the cover of rocks. He couldn't see her for an instant, then saw the flash from her rifle, heard the long burst aimed toward the hillside.

Rourke felt himself smiling—a Russian major leaping to the defense of six U.S. military personnel. "Paul—we're heading down—into the valley."

"Gotchya, John!"

Rourke glanced behind him once, the younger man nearly up alongside him as Rourke rammed a fresh thirty-round magazine up the CAR-15's well. Then he started to run, shouting to Rubenstein, "Paul—give that counterfeit rebel yell of yours!"

He heard it, laughing as he ran, heard the younger man almost scream, "Yahoo!"

The brigands dotting the hillside were starting to shift from their positions now, getting up, running, trapped in a three-way crossfire as Rourke opened up, hearing the rattle of Rubenstein's subgun behind him and to his right, Natalia's M-16 pouring into them, and at last the six men in the valley maneuvering forward, their M-16s blazing.

The nearest of the brigands was perhaps thirty yards away now, Rourke firing out the CAR-15 into the smaller subgroup, the semi-automatic assault rifle coming up empty. He snatched the twin stainless Detonics pistols from the shoulder rig under his jacket, letting the CAR-15 drop to his side on its sling, his thumbs working back the pistols' hammers. He fired both .45s simultaneously, the 185-grain JHPs thudding into the face of the nearest brigand, the body hurtling back, the head seeming to explode, blood—almost like a cloud—momentarily filling the air around it.

The military personnel from the valley were closing now, the brigands who remained alive trapped—and because of that, Rourke realized, more dangerous than before.

Two brigands came at him in a rush, the nearer of the two making to fire an M-16, the one behind him already discharging a revolver. Rourke threw himself down, firing at an upward angle toward the man with the assault rifle, the body doubling over, toppling forward, the 5.56 mms spraying a steady stream into the ground at the already dead, still falling man's feet. Rourke rolled, trying to acquire the target with the revolver. He heard a burst of automatic weapons fire, the man's body spinning, the revolver roaring fire and the body falling, the gun sagging from the limp hand and into the dirt.

Rourke glanced to his right—Paul Rubenstein with the Schmeisser.

24

Rourke shouted, "Paul—thanks!"

But Rubenstein didn't hear him, Rourke realized, the younger man's subgun already firing again.

Rourke was up now, reaching down for the M-16 locked in the dead man's fist. Rourke tugged at the rifle, the fingers locked on it. Rourke stepped on the hand, crushing the bones, then ripped the rifle from the fingers. Loaded magazines for the assault rifle were stuffed behind the man's belt, Rourke reaching down, grabbing up the three that he saw, buttoning out the empty and ramming a loaded twenty up the well. He preferred thirty-rounders himself, the twenty-round magazines not enough fire-power and the forties he had always suspected of putting too much weight into the magazine well.

The M-16's selector was still on auto and Rourke shifted the muzzle toward the brigands, now locked in gunfire with Rubenstein, Natalia and the advancing military. Rourke shouldered the rifle, firing three-round bursts across the sights, shifting the muzzle from target to target, gunfire starting toward him again as bodies fell and the few still surviving brigands turned their fire against him.

The M-16 emptied on a short burst—only two rounds—and Rourke dumped the magazine, ramming the second twenty up the well, then with the rifle at his hip, started to advance, cutting short bursts of two or three rounds into the still remaining brigands. Natalia's gleaming custom revolvers belched bright bursts of fire, men falling before her, Paul with the Schmeisser in his right hand and the battered blue Browning High Power in his left.

Rourke stopped shooting, the last of the brigand bodies twitching on the ground less than five yards from his feet. Natalia stood, her arms sagged along her thighs, the matched Smiths limp in her hands.

Rourke noticed Paul Rubenstein, the slide locked back,

-open, on the emptied Browning, his right hand emptied of the subgun, the Schmeisser dangling at his side. His right hand held his glasses, and his eyes were closed.

Rourke let out a long, hard breath—a sigh. There was a cigar in his pocket and he took it out, setting down the M-16. He lit the thin, dark tobacco in the blue-yellow flame of the Zippo which bore his initials. For some reason, he momentarily studied the initials—J.T.R. The thought—ridiculous—occurred to him. What if he had been someone else, besides John Thomas Rourke? He smiled as he inhaled the smoke deep into his lungs—had he been a man unskilled at fighting he would have been dead, perhaps even since the Night of The War.

Methodically, automatically, he began moving about the field, examining the bodies, ignoring the U.S. II troopers shuffling with seeming unease nearby. A man of peace—sometimes the price of survival was very high.

# Chapter 5

"So, Dr. Rourke—we came looking for you—that's why we're here. President Chambers and Colonel Reed—"

Rourke looked up from loading the six-round Detonics magazine. "Colonel Reed?"

"President Chambers personally promoted him, sir."

Rourke nodded, then looked back to the magazine, double checking through the witness holes that the magazine was fully charged, the lower hole empty as it should be. He took the Detonics and jacked back the slide, locking it with the slide stop. "So you're Captain Cole—"

"That's right, sir—Regis Cole, recently promoted myself," and the young, green-eyed man smiled.

"Hmmm," Rourke nodded, estimating the man's age at perhaps twenty-five, the five enlisted men with him younger seeming still. Rourke inserted the magazine up the Detonics' well and gave it a reassuring pat on the butt—reassuring to himself that it was seated, then worked the slide stop downward, the slide running forward, stripping the first round. Rourke started to lower the hammer.

"I always carry my .45 with the magazine completely full and a round in the chamber," Cole noted.

"A lot of people do," Rourke almost whispered, inhaling on the cigar in the left corner of his mouth. "But a lot of professional gunmen advocate—or advocated I guess these days—stripping the round for the chamber off the top of the magazine."

"To relieve spring pressure?"

"It helps—but not for that," and Rourke thumbed out the magazine with the release button. "Here," and he pointed to the top round in the magazine. "Notice how it's edged forward just a little—makes for more positive feeding than starting with a magazine where the top round has the case head all the way back against the spine of the magazine. Anyway—always works for me," and Rourke replaced the magazine in the pistol and began securing the Detonics under his left armpit in the holster there. "Why were you looking for me, anyway? What'd Reed want?"

Cole, squatting on the ground beside Rourke and slightly at an angle to him, looked around, then behind him. Natalia and Paul were talking, Paul reloading his Schmeisser's magazines. "I'd rather, ahh—talk a bit more privately, Dr. Rourke," Cole said hoarsely.

"There's nothing I wouldn't trust to Paul or Natalia—"

"She's a Russian, sir?"

"Good for her," Rourke smiled.

"I must insist, sir," Cole said again.

Rourke nodded, then shouted across the rocky area where they were, "Natalia—Paul! The captain's going to tell me something in private—I'll tell you all about it as soon as he's through."

Rourke stood up, Cole's green eyes icy.

"Satisfy you?" Rourke smiled.

"I can impress you into service, Dr. Rourke—and then you'll have to do as I say."

"Draft me?" Rourke laughed, spontaneously. Picking up his CAR-15, the magazines for the weapon reloaded from ammo scrounged from the dead brigands, Rourke stared at Cole. "You can't draft me," and he gestured with the CAR-15. "I'm a conscientious objector."

Rourke started walking off toward the tree line, Cole beside him . . .

Rourke had checked all the bodies, each of the brigands—all men—dead. Natalia had walked beside him for part of the search, saying nothing, their eyes meeting, then finally, the last of the dead looked to, she had said, "It hasn't changed, John. I can't live without you."

Rourke had touched his hands to her face—feeling the warmth of the skin, her cheeks slightly flushed. Her eyes—the incredible blueness of them. "When I look up at the stars at night, I—I find myself—seeing you, thinking about you."

"What will we do?"

She had said the words quietly, then cast her eyes down, his hands still framing her face, his fingers letting her windblown hair brush against them.

"I don't know. It seems—it seems I say that more and more when we talk about you and me. I don't—" He folded the woman into his arms, aware then that Rubenstein was eyeing the U.S. military personnel as they closed in, hearing Rubenstein ramming a fresh magazine into the Schmeisser—just in case.

"My uncle," she said after a moment, her voice barely a whisper, her head against his chest. "There is a note for you—he sent me with it. It is urgent—he sent me with it and he sent my things as well. As if—as if he never expected me to return to—to the KGB. To—to my life. And—and I don't know if I expect to—either. I don't know anything any more. Just that I love you, that you're married—that I want more than anything—even more than us, for you to find them—to find Sarah."

She had stepped away, not looking at him, her words barely audible. "How stupid I am." She'd looked at him again and forced a smile, her eyes wet with tears . . .

Cole had not inspired instant respect, or even liking

29

when he had first introduced himself in that next moment—and in the twenty minutes or so in which they had talked, Rourke's feelings toward the young U.S. II Army captain hadn't changed. As they walked now up the hill and toward the tree line, Rourke found himself analyzing the way Regis Cole spoke more than the words he said.

". . . that nobody else could do the job. Your country needs you, Dr. Rourke."

Rourke stopped walking. "What job is it—that no one else can do?" Rourke spit out the stump of burned, chewed cigar butt, then looked Cole in the eye.

"During a debriefing session—you mentioned to Colonel Reed that you had known Colonel Armand Teal before the war—"

"We shared an igloo together for three nights on a survival exercise. I know him."

"He's the commanding officer of Filmore Air Force Base in Northern California—"

"Hope he can swim," Rourke said soberly.

"We've determined that Filmore survived. It was well above the fault line and the mountain chain there would have protected it from the tidal wave effects when the San Andreas went. And there were only neutron hits there as far as we can ascertain as well—overflights. There even seemed to be some activity, a U.S. flag flying."

"Could be the Russians," Rourke told him.

"Sure—but we've tried contacting the base—interference, static—we can't get through and no one answered when the reconnaissance overflight tried radio contact. If it had been the Commies, they would have answered."

"What's so important about Filmore Air Force Base and Armand Teal—you want me to tell you about him?"

"We want you to talk with him," Cole smiled.

"Go to California? Bullshit!" and Rourke turned and

started walking back down the hillside. He heard the sound of a gun coming out of the leather behind him, wheeled, both Detonics pistols coming into his fists as he dropped into a crouch. He heard the clicking of M-16 bolts, the different sounding rattle of steel as the bolt of Rubenstein's Schmeisser opened.

Cole had a Government Model 1911A1 half out of the leather, letting it roll out of his hand on the trigger guard.

"You put your gun away—or I'll kill you," Rourke hissed at him.

"At least let me explain."

"You wanna explain, I'll be down there—with my friends. You tell me, you tell them. And tell your own people to put their rifles down—or you'll be the first."

Cole said nothing for a moment, then only nodded. Holstering his pistol, he shouted loudly, "As you were!"

Rourke pointed the pistols in his balled-tight fists toward the ground, then lowered the hammers with his thumbs. Every human being had a right to weapons— handguns, rifles, edged weapons—for his own self-defense, the defense of loved ones. Regardless of the unrealistic, immoral laws there had been, regardless of the do-gooders who had tried to make America weaponless and Americans helpless. But no man had the right to impose his will—with a gun or anything else—by force. It was a lesson Cole hadn't yet learned—as Rourke turned his back to the Army captain and started down the hillside again, he felt that somehow Cole would learn the lesson still. The hardest way there was.

31

# Chapter 6

"John!"

Rubenstein. A shout. Rourke picked up the CAR-15 from the sling where it hung, starting to run, leaving the bike in the trees, not quite reaching it before he'd heard the call—the shout.

Rourke stopped on the top of the rise, Natalia and Cole were faced off, Cole reaching out to slap Natalia, Natalia's reflexes taking over, catching the hand at the wrist, her body twisting as she side-stepped, Cole sailing up, forward, rolling over, crashing down onto his back. An assault rifle discharged as Natalia started settling her hands on her hips—too close to the twin stainless .357 Magnums she wore there. One of the troopers' M-16 jumped in his hands; Natalia spun around, both pistols still in the leather, her hands clutching at her abdomen.

"John . . ." It was like a wail as she sprawled forward.

"Natalia—" He'd felt fear before—but never this fear. He started to run. Rubenstein was running too, his Schmeisser covering the six soldiers and their commander. "Natalia!" Rourke screamed it now, feeling the muscles in his arms and back, the tendons in his neck—his eyes—all tightening, his heart pounding in his chest. "Natalia!" He was out of the trees, running toward her, the woman's body writhing on the ground, the soldier with the M-16 stepping toward her, the right foot kicking out at her as Cole moved faster than Rourke thought he could have, the pistol he'd pulled twenty minutes earlier coming from the leather again, the base of the frame this time smashing down, Rubenstein half-wheeling, the Schmeisser falling from limp hands, but the hands grasping out for Cole's throat.

"Get him—alive!" It was Cole's voice.

Rourke wheeled, his CAR-15 coming up, firing a three-round semi-auto burst with the CAR-15, Cole spinning, falling back. Rourke kept going—toward Natalia. He heard the working of the bolts, saw the muzzles raising—four M-16s, pointed at his face.

He stopped, his rifle up and on line with them. "I'm going to the woman—if you try to stop me, I'll kill you."

Rourke started ahead, pushing the muzzles of the rifles aside. He didn't care to look at the man behind him. The man beside Natalia—the one who'd shot her—simply stood beside her, his right foot kicking out again—to check if she were dead, Rourke knew.

Rourke snapped the telescoped butt of the CAR-15 up and out. His body wheeled with it, the metal buttplate at the end of the tubular stock hammering square into the soldier's face. Rourke's right knee smashed up, finding the groin, impacting against the scrotum, the man's bloodied face going white as he fell.

Rourke held his left hand out, palm outward, the five other troopers raising their assault rifles to fire, Rourke holding his aimed toward them. "The woman," Rourke rasped. "Or your deaths—"

Rourke dropped to his knees beside her, her fingers covering her abdomen, the fingers pale, laced, woven together, blood seeping through between them as he rolled her over.

The eyelids fluttered.

"Rourke—Rourke!"

It was Cole.

"Rourke—you fuckin' shot me!"

Rourke began to examine the wound—he himself was on borrowed time with Cole, he knew that; but Natalia's borrowed time was coming due. Had he not been a physician, never seen a gunshot wound—had he never seen death, he knew, he would have recognized it in her face.

"You're goin' with me—for those six missiles. Eighty megatons apiece, Rourke—eighty megatons apiece. The woman's good as dead. You want your Jew friend dead too?"

Rourke looked up for an instant, his eyes flickering across the field toward Cole, Cole's left arm bloodied and limp at his side, but in the right hand the Government Model .45 held steady, the muzzle pointed at Rubenstein's head, Rubenstein moving slowly on the ground, trying to get up.

"Where's your base camp, Cole? How do you contact headquarters?" Rourke began examining Natalia's wound in greater detail, spreading her fingers, but slowly. Sometimes the body is its best defense—were the hands holding in her intestines? Gently, he broke the tight weave of her red and sticky fingers. "Where is it?"

"A submarine—two hours away—maybe three. Nuclear submarine—one of the last ones we could contact. Full complement crew—full medical facilities."

The Retreat, Rourke judged, even if he could get Natalia aboard a bike and ride her there without her bleeding to death, was seven hours away by the fastest route, likely spotted with brigand activity, possibly Soviet Army as well. But the likelihood of meeting with Soviet troops for once did not alarm him. They would have access to blood and the facilities for typing, medivac choppers available on call as well. Without massive transfusions, Natalia would likely die. Even with them—Rourke shuddered. Mechanically, he had counted the number of shots in the burst she had taken. Seven rounds.

34

He heard a moan behind him—the trooper who had shot her, then kicked her—the one Rourke had smashed in the face with the rifle butt, the nose broken and twisted to the side of the face, the lips puffed and gushing blood.

"We keep our guns—we get Natalia the best medical attention available," Rourke called out over his shoulder, his voice low.

"Agreed," Cole snapped. "Then you're coming to Filmore Air Force Base—"

"I didn't say that. I'm taking her to the submarine. And we'd better make it fast. That bullet in your arm should come out before the wound infects seriously. And your trooper here—he could bleed to death too."

He'd need to perform a laparotomy to inspect her abdominal organs. Regardless of where the bullets had actually impacted, there would be the trauma of blast effect to deal with. As he started applying a pressure bandage with materials from his musette bag, he realized the peritoneal cavity and the organs there could be cut to pieces. He recalled reading an adventure novel once where the 5.56mm slug had been referred to as a "tumbler"—and it was that. There had been cases in the warfare in Southeast Asia where limbs had been severed by the buzz sawing effect of the .223.

What he saw of her exposed intestines seemed a very pale tan, almost grey in color—like pieces of underdone sausage in appearance. As he tightened the pressure bandage, he prayed that he could keep her alive until they reached the facilities he'd need to operate. That she wouldn't die.

"Paul—" Rourke called the name but never looked. "Get on your feet—and keep that thing you call a Schmeisser handy. Anything happens to Natalia . . ." Rourke let the sentence hang.

The voice that came back sounded strained—tired, perhaps in pain. "Killing would be too good."

# Chapter 7

Her own children—Michael and Annie—played with Millie, the daughter of the ill-fated Jenkins couple. She smiled at the word—what did "Ill-fated?" mean? Was she ill-fated? The children played with the Mulliner dog, they laughed and ran.

Ill-fated.

John—

She squeezed her thighs tight together, feeling self-conscious suddenly sitting there on the porch steps, smoothing the borrowed blue skirt over her knees and then hugging her knees up against her chest, almost but not quite resting her chin on them.

She studied her hands—the nails were short, shorter than she'd ever kept them. But cycling the slide of a .45—she seemed to remember cycling was the correct word—was hard on the nails. Hers had all but broken and she had filed them down.

But at least underneath the nails she was clean—it had been a long time before she'd been able to keep them clean.

She heard the humming of a song, realizing almost absently that she herself was humming it—a song she had danced to with John. At their wedding. The photo was waterstained, bent, almost unrecognizable. But it was smoothed now inside a Bible in Mary Mulliner's house, in the bedroom Sarah used. And Sarah opened the Bible frequently—not for the words there which Mary Mulliner had told her would comfort her, but for the picture being pressed there. John in his tuxedo, herself in her wedding dress. She smiled—trying to remember how many yards of material had been in the skirt.

She hugged her knees again. It was still early enough in the day—perhaps Mary's son would return with news of successfully contacting U.S. II and finding her husband. How many days had she told herself that?

Again, she contemplated the word "ill-fated"—she had thought of it a great deal.

# Chapter 8

Varakov stood beyond the abandoned astronomy museum, on the spot of land, the rocks beyond it separating him from Lake Michigan. For once it was not too cold, though he had yet to find himself able to describe the lake wind as warm.

"Comrade general?"

General Ishmael Varakov recognized the voice—warm, athletic, resonating—somehow just the thought of Colonel Nehemiah Rozhdestvenskiy made his feet hurt all the more.

"Yes, colonel." He still did not turn around.

"Have there been any private communiques from your niece, Major Tiemerovna, Comrade general?"

"No—she is involved in an operation of the most delicate nature even as we speak."

"The Eden Project, Comrade general? For this is the prerogative of the KGB and a KGB agent involved in research on this matter should be under my direct control rather than that of the Army—"

"I have put her on detached duty to my specific command, colonel—she is responsible only to me. As is the nature of her sensitive mission."

"Infiltrating the American resistance perhaps?"

"Colonel—you can make as many lateral references as you wish—but I will divulge no further information at this time. Suffice it to say, her mission is on behalf of the welfare of all."

"Comrade general—though such an action would grieve me greatly, if no news of the major's activities is forthcoming, I shall be left with no other choice than to contact Moscow."

"I am sure you have already contacted Moscow, colonel—were I in your position, that is exactly what I should do. If Moscow becomes sufficiently worried, I will be contacted regarding the matter. In the meantime—"

"Yes, Comrade general?"

"I come here for a few moments of solitude, colonel—" Varakov began to walk, the wind, he reasoned, drowning out the click of the heels from Rozhdestvenskiy's spit-shined boots.

Varakov repeated the words he had used to describe Natalia's mission—but this time to the wind rather than the commander of the North American KGB—"She is involved in an operation of the most delicate nature." He smiled, his feet hurting though to the point where he was ready to sit down. "Delicate operation indeed."

# Chapter 9

Whole blood—and while hers was being typed, Rourke had coordinated with the ship's doctor, Rourke already working with transfusions for the injured trooper who, like Natalia, but less in real danger, had lost too much blood.

He looked at the name tag on the pharmacist mate's white jacket. "Kelly—get the blood pressure cuff inflated to one hundred millimeters of mercury so I can distend and locate the vessels."

Rourke began the same procedure with the soldier—there had been no time to change the man, Rourke for the first time read his name from the sewn tag on the fatigues. "Henderson—if you can hear me, you son of a bitch, we're gonna save your life now." Rourke secured the velcro closures on the blood pressure cuff, then started pumping air. He ran his hand along the inside of the forearm, selecting a likely looking vein. He pumped up a little more so he wouldn't lose it.

"You ready, Kelly?"

"Yes, Doctor," the pharmacist's mate answered. "I never did a direct transfusion before."

"You'll get the hang of it," Rourke nodded. "Got the tube in?" He looked but didn't wait for an answer. "Secure that with some adhesive tape," then he looked at the donor. An ordinary seaman—his name was White. "Mr. White, I'd be lying if I said this won't hurt at all—kind of a numbing sensation. We're just gonna get a pint or so from you. Afterward, in case I forget—go lie down, get some orange juice into you. And thanks for volunteering."

"Yes, sir," the seaman nodded, not looking at the tube now extending from his arm.

Rourke cranked down the table on which the injured man—Henderson—was lying, to get a better flow. He made the veinapuncture on Henderson's forearm, readying the tube—it was already filling, nearing the end. As it did, Rourke attached the tubing to the needle, his left hand already starting to deflate the blood pressure cuff on Henderson's arm.

"Losing a little pressure in White's blood pressure cuff, Doctor," Kelly murmured.

"Mr. Kelly—then get it back up—I need pressure until we're completed. Sing out and have that next donor ready."

Rourke heard a door opening behind him, glanced over his shoulder—it was the ship's doctor—He tried to remember the name. Milton, he thought.

"Doctor Rourke—we typed her at 0 positive—lucky for her it wasn't a negative RH factor. I'm getting as many five hundred milliliter size transfusion bags made up as I can."

"You've got filters for clot removal?" Rourke asked automatically.

"Yes—we're getting the tubing ready now as soon as we wheel her in."

Kelly again. "Doctor—Doctor Rourke I mean—we're at twenty drops per minute—"

"Hold the rate of transfusion there for ten minutes." There was more noise behind him, then he noticed Doctor Milton was gone.

Rourke glanced at the clock on the wall—he gave Natalia another fifteen minutes at best. "Doctor Milton," he shouted. "She ready yet?"

He heard the door open behind him into the smaller of the two surgery rooms.

"Yes—just now, Doctor Rourke."

"Why don't you finish up this man—Kelly's set for the next donor." Rourke moved aside, letting Milton take over for him, walking toward the swinging door, another pharmacist's mate there, scrubbed, helping Rourke as he degloved, then regloved.

"I'm getting started stitching this man's lips," Milton called out.

"I'll begin work then," Rourke nodded, not looking. He stepped into the second and larger surgery. Two men with medical training attended the table, neither of them a surgical nurse, neither really a pharmacist's mate either. "Get that pharmacist's mate—Kelly—get him in here quick," Rourke called out, again not looking—his eyes were riveted on Natalia. He knew it was anesthesia working on her now—that she wasn't dead—not yet.

He approached the operating table, hearing the door swing to behind him.

"It's Kelly, Doctor."

Rourke nodded. "Let's start those transfusion bags." He glanced at the chart Milton had begun, then at Natalia's blood pressure—it was falling too fast.

# Chapter 10

"What's the name of this boat anyway?"

"Well, Mr. Rubenstein—you've got the terminology right. We call her a boat. I guess calling her a "her" is kinda dumb—but it's tradition. She's the U.S.S. *John Paul Jones*."

"How'd you know my name?" Rubenstein asked the older man sitting across from him at the officer's mess table. Rubenstein looked at the radiation badge he'd been given as soon as he'd come aboard. No name appeared on it.

"My business to know everything that goes on aboard this boat—" The man smiled, extending his hand. "I'm Bob Gundersen—Commander Gundersen, sort of an affectionate title the men use with me. Sometimes they just call me Captain, though."

Rubenstein took the hand—it was warm, dry—solid.

"My friends call me Paul, Commander."

"Paul it is then—"

Rubenstein wished again he'd not given up smoking years earlier. "If you know everything that goes on on this ship, then tell me how Natalia's doing?"

"Major Tiemerovna?" He glanced at his watch—Rubenstein noticed it was a Rolex like Rourke wore. "Dr. Rourke started transfusing blood into her about ten minutes ago. He may be operating by now—I don't know that."

"I wish John weren't—"

"Doctor Rourke?"

"Yeah—John. I wish he weren't. I remember reading something once that doctors aren't supposed to operate on family members—or people they're close to. Too much of a stress situation."

"I asked Doctor Rourke the same thing myself," Gundersen nodded, sipping at his coffee. "He said he'd checked with our doctor—Harvey Milton. Doctor Milton told Rourke he'd never worked on a gunshot wound before. He hadn't. He's fresh out of medical school two years ago and before the Night of The War at least, we didn't have many gunshot wounds in the Navy. Now, of course, we don't really have a Navy at all. All the surface ships are gone or at least gone out of contact. Not many of us in the pigboat fleet left either."

"Pigboats?"

"Old submariner's term—real old. But I'm an old submariner," Gundersen smiled. "Guess that's why it doesn't bother me to use it. Naw, but—ahh—anyway, Dr. Milton never had worked on gunshot wounds before and your friend Doctor Rourke said he had. Guess there wasn't much choice. Bumped into Milton outside the sick bay just before Rourke began transfusing Major Tiemerovna—Milton seemed to think Rourke was good. Only hope Harvey was right."

"Harvey?"

"Doctor Milton's first name—"

"Ohh—oh, yeah," Rubenstein nodded.

"Brought this along—figured you might be needing it. Sometimes the waiting gets harder than the doing." From the seat beside him Gundersen produced a small slab-sided bottle. "Medicinal liquor—I've drunk smoother. But there's more where it comes from," and Gundersen handed Rubenstein the bottle. Rubenstein downed his coffee, twisted open the bottle and poured two fingers into the cup. He offered the bottle to Gundersen. "Never touch the stuff when we're underway."

"What's that mean?"

"We've been underwater and heading north for—" he looked at his wristwatch. "Fifty-eight minutes. They don't really need me up there until we get near the icepack—and that'll be a while yet. Should be tricky—imagine there's been a lot of shifting in the pack since the Night of The War."

"Ice pack?" Rubenstein coughed—the medicinal liquor was strong, burning as he felt it in the pit of his stomach.

"As to the running of the submarine here and the welfare of my crew, I give the orders. But for the actual operation it's Captain Cole's say so. He ordered us underway before they put him out to take out the two slugs in his left arm."

"Ohh, shit," Rubenstein muttered, taking another swallow of the liquor. It burned less this time.

# Chapter 11

A long mid-line incision was made in order to expose the internal organs. Rourke began exploring the stomach.

Dr. Milton's voice sounded nearly as labored as the respirator. "Why are you going through the gastrocolic omentum, Doctor Rourke?"

Mechanically, his mind on his hands and not his words, Rourke answered. "To open the lesser sac of the stomach." The membrane was a loose fold. "Suction" he called, Milton himself assisting. The greater omentum covered the anterior stomach surface and intestines like a drape, Rourke stopping, noting a hematoma at the mesenteric attachment. "We have to evacuate this hematoma." Evacuating, Rourke inspected the stomach wall between the leaves of the greater and lesser omentum. There was damage, a whole bullet, not a fragment, partially severing the connection to the rear wall of the abdomen. "Gotta get that sucker out," Rourke remarked, exhaling hard, feeling ready to collapse. As each bullet or fragment was removed, Rourke carefully repaired the organ damage with continuous locking chromic sutures.

According to the clock on the surgery wall—he supposed bulkhead would be more appropriate since they were on a naval vessel and—likely—already underway, he had spent more than an hour and a half sorting through the mess that was Natalia's stomach, finding bullet fragments and piecing them meticulously together—if he left even the smallest fragment, the complications could be legion—could be mortal.

"Do you have your closing sutures available?"

"You're ready to close her?" Dr. Milton asked.

"No—just thinking ahead—you have what I need?"

"Yes."

"Fine."

"Are you sure there were seven bullets?"

"Yes," Rourke nodded. "Somebody gimme a wipe, huh?"

A hand reached out—he didn't see who it belonged to, his eyes bothering him with the light as well, the glare—he needed a smoke, needed sleep—but Natalia needed life. "Damnit—" Rourke almost spat the word. In the fat of the greater omentum he found what he had not wanted to find. The sixth bullet had been intact—he had hoped that the seventh would be.

It was not.

He had the jacket, the gilding metal—but the core of the bullet—the core had separated and was still somewhere inside her.

As Rourke held it up, trying to determine if anything other than the core itself were missing, Milton asked, "Is that it?"

"Unless a bullet is made of lead alone, it usually has a whole or partial jacket surrounding it. These should be full metal jacketed if they were standard G.I. Ball—and all the others have been. Somehow the jacket peeled away from the lead core and the lead core is missing in there still—and you can see the way the jacket peeled back that it was ripped—a lot of force bearing on it. Looks like there are pinhead-sized fragments of the jacket missing as well. I'll need someone standing by with a microscope so we can piece this thing back together as we go—can't afford to leave any pieces behind."

"I'll get someone on that," Milton murmured.

Rourke closed his eyes for an instant—he thought of the eyes beneath the closed lids beyond the surgical tent. "Natalia," he whispered.

# Chapter 12

Paul Rubenstein had given up on the medicinal liquor—he had no desire to get drunk. And the coffee—good by anyone's standard—had proved too much for him as well—two trips to what he'd rapidly learned was called "the head". He had given up smoking many years before—so he sat now, staring at the wall, wondering. And he knew it wasn't a wall—he remembered editing an article years ago that had dealt with ships and boats and a wall was a bulkhead—he thought.

He wondered if Rourke knew—knew that the ship was underway. He realized that even if Rourke had not been told, he would have suspected as much. And he wondered even more about the welfare of Natalia.

He found himself smiling at mention of her name—that a major in the KGB would have found such a warm place in his heart amazed him still. His parents, not directly involved in the Holocaust, had told him of relatives who had been. The SS, the Gestapo—and he rationally realized that the KGB was essentially the same. But the woman—she was different.

If he felt such torture waiting for the outcome of the operation—six hours had passed since it had begun—he could not even imagine what it was Rourke himself felt. A slip of the knife, a misjudgment and a woman that Rourke obviously loved would be dead. Rubenstein shivered—not with cold.

He sat bolt upright. "The operation's over."

He turned around—it was Rourke. "John—is—"

She was dead, Rubenstein thought—otherwise—

"She should make it," Rourke nodded, his face haggard-looking, leaner seeming than Paul had ever seen it. Under the most bizarre conditions, Rubenstein had secretly marveled that Rourke always found the time to stay clean shaven when there was sufficient water available to do so. But now, his face was stubbled, deep lines etched there heightened by the shadow of beard.

"You look like hell," Paul said quietly.

"Matches the way I feel—the last bullet. Nine fragments, some of them almost as small as the head of a pin. Had to reconstruct it under a microscope. Made me realize the last time I performed major surgery was a long time ago. The hands are just as steady, but the reflexes I'd learned weren't there."

"We're underway—like they call it. You know that," the younger man told him.

"I felt it—yeah."

"What are we going to do, John?"

"If I got everything and did everything right, Natalia could be up and around in about a week. We can't do anything until then. You meet the captain?"

"Commander Gundersen—yeah—seems okay."

"It's Cole we've gotta worry about—those orders of his—something doesn't sound right about them."

"He wants to start a nuclear war all over again? That's crazy."

"I'm going to see if there's some way this Commander Gundersen can contact President Chambers or Reed. But in the meantime, we're stuck."

"Gundersen's men took my guns—I didn't see any way of arguing it—six of them and no running room."

Rourke nodded soberly. "I took off my pistols when I scrubbed—most of them anyway," and Rourke smiled.

"But you were right—trying a shootout in a metal skin in the water—under it now—would have been stupid."

"You're not gong through with this—to find the missiles. Are you?"

"I don't have much choice. We'll be there anyway when this thing surfaces—and if I can contact Chambers and he confirms that Cole is acting in his behalf, then I'll have to. And if I can't contact Chambers—my gut still tells me there's something wrong. Something really wrong with Cole and his outfit. And if Cole is some kind of crazy—or maybe a Russian Natalia wouldn't have known about—or something else—we can't let him get his hands on those six missiles. He was talking about them—eighty megaton capacity for each missile. Nearly five hundred megatons combined."

"What started it between Cole and Natalia?" Rubenstein asked.

Rourke sat down, holding his head in his hands for a moment, then looked up. He picked up the bottle of medicinal liquor—"Looks like it tastes great."

"You get used to it," and Rubenstein felt himself smile.

"Yeah—well—after Natalia's suction has been working for a while—"

"Her what?"

"Got a Levin tube suctioning her until peristalsis resumes—but there's always a chance the suture line I made wasn't complete enough and I might have to open her up again—I should know in about six hours or so—gonna try and sleep."

"I could feel for you, John—doing that—holding her life in your hands."

"A lot of things I've been thinking about lately," and Rourke smiled. "I always get the impression you look to me as the problem solver—don't you?"

Embarassed slightly, Rubenstein only nodded.

"Well—if I'm so smart, how the hell come I'm in love

with my wife and I'm in love with Natalia at the same time, huh?''

Rourke said nothing else, reaching into his shirt pocket and taking one of the dark tobacco cigars and lighting it, his face more lined and tired than before.

# Chapter 13

Sarah Rourke opened her eyes, her eyes, her face warm in the shafts of brilliant sunlight coming through the screened open window, the curtains blowing softly in the warm breeze. She sat up in bed, rubbing her eyes once, then stretching, feeling too warm in the nightgown.

"Spring," she smiled. She had inured herself to the insanity of the seasons since the Night of The War. Today it would be spring—tomorrow it might be winter again. "Tomorrow—" She laughed as she said the word.

She pushed down the sheet and the quilt and swung her legs over the side of the bed, standing up, barefoot, the nightgown's hem hiding her feet. She walked to the window. There was quiet—the dog not running madly with the children yet. She would shower later, she told herself.

She stepped away from the window, standing near the dresser, conscious of herself as she pulled the nightgown over her head and put it on the bed. She looked at herself—her breasts weren't exactly little anymore. Nursing two children had seen to that. But there was, as best she could tell, barely an ounce of fat on her body—the constant running, fighting—all of it since the Night of The War had seen to that.

She wondered absently—taking a bra from the dresser drawer and starting to put it on—if time in the future would be reckoned from the Night of The War—like it had been since the birth of Christ?

The irony was not lost on her.

Peace versus war.

She stepped into her panties, dismissed the idea of wearing a slip and pulled the yellow dress from the hook inside the wardrobe cabinet doors and took it from the hanger. She pulled the dress on over her head, starting to button the back of the dress mechanically, without watching, as she stared out the window. It would be a beautiful day—perhaps so beautiful that Mary Mulliner's son would come back and bring word of contacting John—that he was well, that he was coming for her and for the children.

She began to brush her hair, her hair longer than she had kept it in years—somehow she was unwilling to cut it. She set down the brush, opened the top drawer of the dresser and began to search for a pony tail holder to keep her hair back from her face. The old blue T-shirt she had worn—it was washed, folded neatly—She looked under it. The terminally rusted .45 her husband had left for her, that she had carried next to her abdomen since the Night of The War.

She picked it up, her reflexes automatic now as she pushed the magazine release catch button, dropping the magazine on the bed clothes, then with her stronger right hand, the gun held in her left, drew back the Government Model's slide.

The Colt's chamber was empty. She knew it would be—but had learned never to trust to that.

She pointed the emptied gun at a safe space of exterior wall and snapped the trigger, the hammer falling with a loud "click", an infinitesimal amount of oil felt sprayed on the web of her hand as the hammer fell.

"My God." She simply shook her head, looking at the pistol; the sunlight and the yellow dress she wore somehow no longer the same to her.

# Chapter 14

Rourke saw them—Michael and Annie. They were running—but running happily. There was a beach—they were running along it in the surf, barefooted, their pants legs rolled up but still hopelessly wet as the foaming water lapped against their shins, the children only half-heartedly running.

He looked at himself—the weight distribution of his shoulder rig felt odd to him and he lifted his shoulders under it, searching the beach—Sarah had to be there too.

He wanted to shout to Michael and Annie—but even more than holding them he wanted to watch them run—to play. Hear them laugh. Annie had grown—but somehow she hadn't changed at all. The wild-eyed little kid—the happy girl, the girl who made you laugh. He laughed at himself.

Sarah—he still couldn't see her.

He watched Michael—his face was more serious than it had been—tanned more deeply than it always seemed to be, even in the dead of winter. He was somehow taller and straighter than he'd been just before the Night of The War, and even disguised under the T-shirt Michael wore, he could see the boy's musculature—how it had changed, matured.

Rourke stopped, seeing someone lying further along the beach. He brought the Bushnell 8x30s out and focused them. The figure was a woman, wearing a bathing suit—she lay sunning herself, pale seeming under the bright sun on the sand.

"Sarah," he whispered. He started to run, the binoculars bouncing against his chest as they swung from their strap. "Sarah!" The children would hear him he knew.

The sand was hard to run in, slowing him. "Sarah!"

He was there suddenly, beside her. She didn't turn around.

"Sarah—I tried to make it back sooner—you'll never know how I tried. There were so many battles to fight—and—"

She didn't answer. She didn't move. He dropped to his knees in the sand. The body was so familiar to him—the patterns of the tiny freckles on her shoulders, the way she pushed her hair from the nape of her neck when she lay in the sun.

The flesh was cold as he touched it.

"Sarah—" He drew his hand back, then touched gently against her back. Still cold—clammy to the touch.

Swallowing hard, feeling his muscles bunching tight, he bent closer to her and felt at the neck for a pulse. There was none.

"Oh, Jesus," he rasped.

He took his hands away for a moment, then placed them both on the shoulders, turning the body.

Michael and Annie were standing beside him.

"Why didn't you come," Michael asked, his voice serious sounding, hurt sounding—like Rourke had heard it when he had been too busy to play, too busy to talk. "Why didn't you come, Daddy?"

Rourke couldn't answer—he knew they wouldn't understand.

"Your mother," he whispered, then looked back at the face as he finished rolling over the body.

Dead.

Lids open—the eyes a brilliant blue.

"Natalia." He heard himself whisper it.

Annie said. "That's why Daddy didn't come, Michael."

He turned to look at the children, to say, "No—that's not right—" But they were running off toward the surf again, laughing.

But the laughter somehow sounded forced to him, hollow.

It was Sarah's body as he drew it into his arms, but somehow Natalia's face and he asked himself if he were insane.

"What—"

"John!"

"Michael—please understand—"

"John!"

"Damnit!" Rourke opened is eyes, light in a yellow shaft coming through from the companionway. The face over him, shaking him—Paul.

"John—you all right—you were—"

"What's the matter?"

"That's why I came, John—it's Doctor Milton—he says Natalia's dying."

Rourke sat up.

"Michael," he murmured. Then he pushed himself from the cot and started into the companionway, Rubenstein beside him.

# Chapter 15

"I won't let you die." He told her that even though she couldn't hear him.

"Doctor Rourke—"

"I'm opening her again. Maybe I counted wrong and there was another fragment that didn't show up—"

"But she's bleeding to death."

"I'm opening her."

"Later maybe—you could—"

"If I don't—you want me to run down the list of what could happen and what would happen first—"

"Let me—you look exhausted."

"No—no," and Rourke felt himself shaking his head. "No." He looked at his hands, then touched them to her face . . .

"We're going to have a couple members of the crew down for the count—I've had men volunteer to give a second pint of blood—I'm taking half pints only."

"Give me their names when this is through," Rourke told Milton. "If she makes it she'll want to thank them." It wasn't the suture line—it was gastric bleeding and as Rourke completed re-opening her he could see nothing. "I need suction here—fast—there's so much fluid I can't—"

"Coming up." It was Kelly and Rourke nodded, starting to apply the suction. At the rate at which she was bleeding—he didn't finish the thought . . .

"Here—" and Rourke glanced at the clock—it had

been more than eighty minutes. "You—you close her," and Rourke stepped back, blood half way up his forearms, staining his gown, his gloved hands splotched with it—her blood. He stripped away the gloves.

"Here, Doctor—" It was Kelly.

"No—no—you stick with Doctor Milton—I'm all right." Rourke couldn't leave the room—he was too tired, his head aching too badly. On the white clothed tray was the bullet. He picked it up—there had been eight rounds, this one buried in the abdominal wall—a place he'd searched and missed before. Upon removing the bullet, he controlled the bleeding with another continuous locked chromic suture. "Tired," he murmured.

He started to strip away the gown and when it was half off, dropped the bullet in the pocket of his pants—it would remind him of two things, always—mortality and fallability. And a third thing—to persevere.

# Chapter 16

Sarah, her hands stabbed into the squared pockets of her dress, walked. She felt the high grass against her bare legs, felt the sun warm her chest and back. She was changing—she knew that, had realized it from the first time she'd picked up her husband's gun when they'd left the house on the Night of The War. Known the change was irreversible since she'd shot the brigands that morning after. She had killed.

She had killed many times since then and no longer did she vomit in her first moment alone afterward.

Almost absently, she wondered if John had changed. Always his guns, his knives, his obsession with being prepared. For what she had never understood—and now she understood. Was he at his Retreat—would she ever find it? Would he ever find her?

She stopped, standing midway in the long field made narrow by the natural foundation of the ground, a ridge crest at its far end, trees there rising to the higher ground beyond the shallow valley. She saw movement. Before the Night of The War, it would only have been the movement of a bird, perhaps a squirrel who'd misjudged his weight and landed on a branch too weak to support him—but the movement now she saw as something else—the branch had bent low.

She listened, feeling it in the stray wisps of hair that had not gotten caught up in the rubber band-like pony tail holder which held her hair. Her fists knotted in the pockets of her dress. She licked her lips.

Movement again—a man.

She stood there, assessing her options, finding herself coldly professional about them, smiling as she thought again of the change in herself.

Two hundred yards at least to the end of the field, the ground slightly uneven but runnable for her. Another hundred yards or more from the edge of the field to the house. There was an AR-15 beside the door of the kitchen. If she could get that far.

She cursed herself for being stupid and leaving the house—so far from it—without a gun.

"Sarah," she whispered to herself. She turned and started walking, not too slowly, but slowly enough that she hoped no one would think she had spotted the movement in the trees.

It might only be the returning resistance fighters—but they wouldn't hide in the trees.

It might be Soviet forces moving through—she doubted that. They traveled with greater fanfare.

Brigands.

A woman caught alone in the open—she couldn't lie to herself as to her fate if they got her. She had seen what they did to women, to little girls—even to little boys. But to women most of all.

She felt a pain in her, below her abdomen. She would have put the twinge down to ovulation—but it was fear instead.

She quickened her pace, snatching up a piece of high grass in her hands and using that as an excuse to turn around.

Men—six, then six more, then more than a dozen others. There seemed to be more each time she shifted her gaze. She watched them—they watched her. Big—long haired, some of them. The clothes, the weapons—

61

"Brigands." She whispered the word to herself.
Then she screamed it. "Brigands!"
Sarah Rourke started to run.

# Chapter 17

Her heart pounded in her chest, her lungs aching with the oxygen deprivation, the skirt of her yellow dress bunched against her thighs, the wind resistance as she ran keeping it there. She heard the sounds behind her—motorcycles.

She turned, starting to look at the brigands pursuing her, her right foot catching in a clump of the high grass that was somehow tangled. She felt herself falling.

Her chest, her face—she slapped into the sandy ground.

She looked behind her as she jerked her right foot free—there were three men on bikes, closing fast. She could hear them shouting now above the roar of their engines.

"A woman—shit!"

She pushed herself to her feet, scooping up two handfuls of the sandy soil. Then she started running again. Fifty yards remained to the end of the field and there was nothing she could do to outrun the men on the bikes.

Sarah stopped, turning, her fists bunched tight together. The lead biker slowed, the other two slowing behind him.

"Ya'll git tired a runnin', woman?"

"Maybe," she gasped, nodding.

"Hey—maybe I like my women when they skin sweats—maybe I'll just put me a rope 'round yo neck and run ya awhiles, huh? See how ya like it and git ya t'beg me maybe to stop. Maybe offer me something good, huh?''

Sarah said nothing.

The man dismounted the bike, the engine still throbbing. She had ridden a bike with John but counted herself no expert. But only two hundred, maybe two hundred and fifty yards to the house—it as her only prayer.

The brigand, his face dripping dirty sweat, the sweat running in brown rivulets along his neck and hair-covered chest, stopped, less than a yard from her. He reached out his right hand—she felt it explore her neck, start to knot into her hair.

She took a single step, closer to him, thrusting both hands up and outward into his eyes, the sandy dirt powdering through her splayed fingers, the man starting to scream. Her nails were too short for it, but she dug them into the eyes, the man grabbing at her as she smashed her bare right knee up into his crotch.

There was a pistol—she felt it as he sagged against her—and she snatched it from his waistband. She almost lost the gun, the grips sweaty and wet. An automatic.

She lifted the pistol into her left hand as she stepped back, the man screaming, pawing at her as he sank to his knees. Her right hand worked back the slide, her eyes catching sight of the flicker of brass in the sunlight—there had already been a round chambered.

The two closest bikers were starting toward her.

She let the slide go forward and fired, the pistol bucking in her hands, but the shot low. She didn't see it impact. She fired again, the nearest biker less than two yards from her.

She saw the explosion of blood on his upper chest just under the hollow of the neck.

She stepped back, firing again at the second biker, the man's right arm leaving the handlebars, the right hand grasping at the abdomen, the bike starting to go down.

There was a hand on her ankle, dragging her down. As she fell forward, she fired again, the pistol discharging point blank into the face of the first man still on the ground.

The hand was still locked on her ankle. She fired the pistol—it was a .45 but smaller than her husband's gun somehow. The shot impacted into the forearm, the hand's grip on the bare flesh of her ankle loosening.

She tripped, caught herself and fired a wild shot toward the remainder of the brigand force, the men halfway across the field, some on bikes, some on foot, some pickup trucks coming behind them, packed with men and some women—all armed.

The first brigand's bike was the only one still standing near her, the engine still pulsing loudly. She ran for it, straddling it, her underpants feeling the wetness of sweat on the saddle as the wind gusted, billowing her skirt.

She fumbled the controls, hoping she wouldn't by accident shut the machine off.

It started to lurch ahead, the pistol thrown down because she didn't have any place to hold it, her fists locked white-knuckle tight on the handlebars, the machine too powerful for her, she realized, the movement of the fork as she started across the field tearing at her muscles, making her shoulders ache.

She wasn't sure she knew how to stop it.

There was gunfire coming from the house—either Mary Mulliner or the hired man Mary had taken in—perhaps Michael. "Michael," she gasped. Were Michael and Annie still in the house?

She heard the light, intermittent reports of the AR-15—whoever was firing the gun didn't know how to handle it, wasn't as good as—

"As good as I am," she screamed into the wind.

She could hear the brigand bikes all around her behind her.

She kept moving, out of the field and across the yard now, the house looming up ahead of her coming fast—too fast.

She started trying to find the brakes, the machine slowing but not fast enough.

She was losing it. She gave the brakes all she had and threw herself from the machine as it skidded in the grass near the back door leading to the kitchen.

She rolled, her hands and knees tearing on the dirt and gravel mixed in with the grass. She rolled again, the biker nearest behind her sailing up into the air, his bike going out of control as it bounced over the bike she'd jumped clear of.

The man's body was still in the air, there was a scream. The body hammered through the kitchen window over the sink.

Sarah pushed herself up, a biker starting for her. The washbasket was beside her. She threw it at him. He kept coming. She was running, toward the back door. A rake—the heavy one with the long metal tines that Mary used for her vegetable garden on the side of the house—leaned by the kitchen door.

Sarah reached for it, grabbed it, the biker closing.

She swung the rake, the tines catching the brigand biker full in the face.

There was a scream and she thought she felt blood spraying her hands and arms.

The biker collapsed from his machine.

Sarah half threw herself up the steps and through the doorway.

Mary was firing the AR-15.

"Give it to me!" Sarah snatched it from Mary's hands, ramming the flash deflectored muzzle through a pane of unbroken glass.

Two shot semi-automatic bursts—she started firing. One biker down, another biker.

66

"Sarah!"

She heard the scream. She turned. The biker who'd sailed through the window was conscious, starting to crawl up from the sink top, reaching for a pistol.

Sarah grabbed the butcher knife on the counter and hammered it down—into the back of the biker's neck. The brigand was dead, blood gushing out of his open mouth past his tongue.

She looked at the far kitchen wall—Michael and Annie and the little Jenkins girl.

"Michael—keep low—get my rifle and my pistol from upstairs—hurry—then find anything else you can."

She didn't wait for an answer, pumping more shots at the brigands streaming into the yard.

"Mary—search that dead man for guns and ammunition—we'll need it all!"

Sarah—she thought of it as she pulled the trigger for a fast shot on a brigand biker, seeing the man's hands fly to his face where she'd shot him. She had changed.

# Chapter 18

He had lost all sense of day and night—he awoke now, realizing that on the East Coast where he had last seen land it would be mid-morning. He frowned at the luminous dial of the Rolex, then sat up in the darkness.

A nuclear submarine—he tried recalling how much actual time had gone by. Not expert when it came to submarines, he wondered if they had gone under the ice yet. He doubted it though.

Sarah and the children—somewhere in Georgia or the Carolinas, perhaps as far as Alabama or Mississippi, or perhaps again up in Tennessee.

"Up in Tennessee," he laughed.

He reached over and flipped on the light. He rubbed his stubbled cheeks—he needed a shave, badly—and he could smell his own body.

"All right," he mumbled to himself, sighing heavily. It was time to do something.

John Rourke stood up. "Time to do something," he murmured . . .

He felt naked as he walked the companionway looking for Paul Rubenstein—no guns. It was the first time since the Night of The War—except for periods of captivity under the Russians and the problem with the woman in the town who had chosen suicide—that he had been without them. As he turned what he would have called a corner, his hair still wet from the shower, picking his way

68

over the lintel of one of the myriad watertight doors, an officer—a lieutenant JG stopped him.

"You're Doctor Rourke?"

"Yes," Rourke nodded.

"The captain requested that you join him on the bridge, sir. I can take you there."

Rourke nodded again, falling into step behind the young man. "How is the Soviet major doing, sir?"

Rourke smiled—it was hard to think of Natalia Anastasia Tiemerovna as "the Soviet major." He let out a long sigh. "She's doing fine, lieutenant. Still weak, but she's sleeping normally. Should be for a while. Sort of the body's natural defense mechanism against things like what happened to her."

"That's good to hear, sir," the lieutenant nodded, Rourke watching the back of his head as the man ducked. "She's got a pint of my blood in her."

Rourke told him, "I thought your face looked familiar—you were from the second time around."

"You got it, sir—guess it was more than a pint. Boy, did I sack out last night."

Rourke laughed. "Yeah—so did I. And I didn't even give blood. What's Commander Gundersen want to see me about?" Rourke asked, ducking his head for another watertight door.

"Don't know, sir," the young man answered. "Here we are," and the lieutenant stepped through into a compartment that seemed almost too spacious to be believed aboard a submarine, nuclear or not. Rourke had several times been aboard the post-World War II diesel subs, their forward and aft torpedo rooms the only large areas to be found. The spaciousness of the operating theater had surprised him—was not nearly so surprising as the quarters he'd been given. Like the size of a rather large bathroom as opposed to the subminiature closet-sized offices and quarters on the earlier subs. He had ridden nuclear subs before, but never for any length of time, and these in his days in CIA Covert Operations.

This nuclear sub was apparently of the newest class, the ones begun just prior to the Night of The War. It was at the least the size of a decent tonnaged destroyer, perhaps larger. He stood now, overlooking the maze of lights and panels, the many crew members.

He was impressed.

"Like my bridge, Doctor Rourke?" Commander Gundersen sounded confident, assured—appreciative of Rourke's stare.

"I'm going to build one just like this soon as I get home—got a kit?" Rourke smiled.

"I understand the Soviet major—"

"Natalia Tiemerovna."

"Yes—understand she's going to be fine."

Rourke nodded, still surveying the bridge before entering it. "Always the risk of a low grade infection with surgery so massive, but yes—I think so."

"Will she fully recover—I mean—"

"Yeah—yeah," Rourke nodded again. "Matter of fact, she should be pretty much back to normal in a week or so. Still a little weak, but normal."

"Good—I'm glad to hear that—come down."

Rourke nodded, stepping away from the watertight door and taking one long stride across the metal platform, then taking the ladder down to the core of the bridge. Gundersen stood at its center, hands resting on the periscope housing. His fingers tapped at it—not nervously, but expectantly.

Gundersen turned to his side, "Charlie—take her up to periscope depth."

"Aye, Captain," a voice sang back.

There was a muted humming, Rourke feeling nothing in the way of movement.

"Periscope depth, sir," the same voice called out.

"Good, Charlie—let's take a look here. Sonar give me a readout on anything that gets near us."

"Aye, sir," another voice called.

The periscope tube raised, Gundersen flipping out the handles on its sides. "Always like to take a look at the pack before we go under—wanna look yourself, Doctor?"

Rourke stepped toward the periscope—noticing now it was the largest of several. He stepped nearer as Gundersen stepped back and turned the periscope handles toward him.

Rourke pressed his eyes to the subjective lenses, his nose crinkling at the faint but distinctive smell of the rubber eye cups. "Makes you want to say 'Torpedo Los,' doesn't it?" Rourke said, studying the white rim at the far edge of his vision—the icecap.

He heard Gundersen laugh. "First civilian I've ever met with the guts to say that—it does make you want to say that the first time. Crank her around back and forth a little and take a look at the world before we go under."

Rourke only nodded, turning the periscope slowly. Massive blocks of ice floated everywhere in the open water leading in the distance to the edge of the icepack. Small waves—wind whipped Rourke judged—would momentarily splash the objective lens. Without looking away, he asked, "Has there been as much change in the icepack as you'd suppose?"

"Another good remark, Dr. Rourke. Apparently a great deal of change."

Rourke stepped back from the periscope, looking at Gundersen. "Spreading?"

"Rapidly—I mean we can't really measure with any sophistication now because all the satellites are gone. But as best we can judge the icepack is advancing."

"That's just marvelous," Rourke nodded. He leaned back on the side of an instrument console.

"Down periscope," Gundersen ordered, flipping the

handles up. "Ed—you've got the con. I'd say take her down a little more than we normally do and ride herd on the ice machine—split the shifts so the operators will keep on their toes."

"Prepare to blow," a man standing opposite Gundersen ordered. "Rig for full negative."

"Aye, sir," a crewmen called back.

Gundersen stepped up to Rourke. "Doctor—like to join me in my cabin—talk a bit?"

"Fine," and Rourke followed Gundersen out. They walked the way Rourke and the lieutenant JG had come, turning off into a cabin with a wooden door, the lettering there reading, "Commander Robert Gundersen, Captain."

"Got my name on the door and everything," Gundersen smiled, holding the door for Rourke. As Rourke entered the cabin he realized it was actually two cabins—Gundersen's office with a decent-sized desk comprised the main cabin and there was a door off to Rourke's left as he faced the desk—sleeping quarters? Rourke decided that they were.

"Sit down, Doctor," Gundersen said, nodding toward a couch on the far interior wall.

Rourke said nothing, but started toward the couch.

"Coffee?" Gundersen asked, pouring into a large mug from a hotplate on the bookcase behind his desk.

"Sure," Rourke answered. "Mind if I smoke?"

"No—we can scrub the air. Go ahead."

Rourke took one of his small, dark tobacco cigars from the pocket of his blue chambray shirt, found the Zippo in the pocket of his jeans and rolled the striking wheel under his thumb.

"Where do you find lighter fluid?"

"Gasoline, usually—lighter fluid currently."

"Thought I recognized a survivor in you. Here," and Gundersen handed Rourke a truck-stop sized white mug,

72

the coffee steaming hot and smelling good as Rourke sipped at it. "So," Gundersen sighed, sitting down opposite Rourke in a small leather chair. "You're the man everybody was so hot to find. Ex-CIA, I understand."

"Yeah," Rourke nodded, inhaling on his cigar, then exhaling a cloud of gray smoke. He watched as the ventilation system caught it, the smoke dissipating rapidly.

"And the president needed you."

"That's what Cole tells me," Rourke nodded.

"That's what he tells me too."

"Where'd you bump into Cole?" Rourke asked suddenly.

"We'd been surfacing at nights, trying to make contact with a U.S. base—stumbled onto the U.S. II frequency after threading our way through a lot of Russian, if you know what I mean. With the satellites gone, the laser communication network was out. Just luck I guess."

"Did you talk with President Chambers?"

"Spoke with a guy named Colonel Reed—all in code. Never really spoke at all. You know. But he was named on the communiques—all Reed under orders from Chambers. Said they were sending out a man named Cole and a small patrol for an urgent mission we could help with." Gundersen laughed. "Didn't have anything else to do. Fired all our missiles. All we had left were torpedoes—no enemy submarines around to shoot 'em at. I think most of the Soviet Fleet that wasn't destroyed is fighting in the Mediterranean."

"Used to be a beautiful part of the world," Rourke nodded.

"Used to be—not now. It's a bloodbath over there—and a lot of radiation, I understand. You know, being a submarine commander and having a nuclear war—I feel like that guy in the book."

"But this isn't Australia," Rourke smiled.

"No—but I wonder. The icepack advancing—understand the weather up above," and he jerked his thumb upward, "has been pretty screwy. End of the world?"

"Maybe," Rourke shrugged.

"You said that awful casually," Gundersen said, lighting a cigarette.

"Yeah—maybe I did. If it is, I can't stop it. Just try to survive it after I find my family."

"Wife and two children, right?"

"Right," Rourke answered. "What are Cole's orders?"

"Pretty much like I imagine he told you. Find this air base if it is still there—supposed to be. We get you in as close as we can, then shanks mare all the way and Cole uses whatever available transportation there is to get the warheads out and back to the submarine. Then we deliver them to U.S. II Headquarters or wherever—that last part hasn't been spelled out yet. I guess it will be."

"What do you do after that?"

"I don't know. Keep going. We can run for a long time yet—a long time. Provisions should hold up for a long time as well. Then I guess we'll die like everybody else if the world ends. I don't know. Can't plan too far in advance these days."

"What do you think about Cole?"

"He's a prick—but he's got the President's signature on his written orders. I can't argue with that."

"Do you trust him?"

"No—but he's got orders and I'm supposed to help him carry them out. I disarmed you and your Mr. Rubenstein simply to keep the peace. We get topside, regardless of what Cole says, I'll re-arm you both. Can't have you guys shooting holes in my submarine, though—my engineer complains like an old lady about it. See," and Gundersen jerked his thumb upward again, smiling, "the roof leaks."

"Ohh," Rourke nodded. "Wouldn't have suspected that."

Gundersen laughed, leaning forward, gesturing with his cigarette. "To answer your question before you ask—I've got no plans at all for Major Tiemerovna. She's a pretty woman—I think the guys giving blood and everything to keep her alive pretty much caused my crew to look at her that way, not as a Communist agent. She minds her manners once she's up and around and as far as I'm concerned, she's free as a bird. I understand she was pretty heroic herself when—the Florida thing. Jesus—" and Gundersen inhaled hard on the cigarette, the tip glowing brightly near the flesh of his yellowed first finger and thumb.

"Yeah—she was. Saved a lot of American lives. Saved a lot of lives period."

"I'm not planning to rearm Major Tiemerovna, though—I realize she's a loyal Russian and I guess that's just as it should be. And I'm not inviting her unescorted onto the bridge, into the torpedo rooms, the reactor room—anywhere sensitive. Couldn't risk her opening a torpedo tube on us and sending us to the bottom. Not that I'm saying necessarily that she would."

"She would if she had to," Rourke smiled.

"Exactly—but beyond that, I don't care what Cole wants. She stays on my ship, my word's the law here, not his."

"Thank you," Rourke nodded.

"I got a present for you—figured you might use it—I can't anymore."

Gundersen got up, walked across his room to his desk and sat down behind it. Rourke stood up, following him, stopping then in front of the desk. From a large locked drawer, Gundersen produced a black leather pouch, snapped closed with a brass fitting. He opened the pouch—inside it were six Detonics stainless magazines, the magazines empty as Rourke looked more closely, the magazines ranked side by side, floorplates up.

"I've seen these," Rourke commented, shifting the cigar along his teeth into the left corner of his mouth.

"It's called a 'Six Pack'—Milt Sparks made 'em before the Night of The War. Mostly for Government Models, but I had him make one for my Detonics. But then I lost the gun—it fell out of my belt and went overboard. Without the gun, the magazines are useless. So, unless I can trade you out of one of yours, you may as well have it."

"Thank you," Rourke nodded, turning the heavy black leather Six Pack over in his hands. "You can't trade me out of one of my Detonics pistols."

"Sort of figured that—use it in good health—ha," and Gundersen laughed.

Rourke got the joke.

# Chapter 19

John Rourke sat quietly, listening. What he listened to was the regular sound of Natalia's breathing. She was still sleeping. He had sat beside the bed for nearly an hour, ever since leaving Gundersen. Paul was being shown about the submarine—Rourke had postponed the grand tour until later. He had wanted to think, and the quiet of Natalia's room in sick bay had been the best place, he'd thought.

What would happen when he found Sarah and the children?

He had not thought of an answer—for over the weeks since the Night of The War and his meeting with Natalia he had formed new bonds, in some ways stronger bonds than he had ever had. There was Paul Rubenstein—once a man who could do nothing for himself, now a man who could do most things—and most things well. There was Natalia herself—Rourke looked at her, her eyelids fluttering. She was awakening.

He stood up, walked to beside her bed and touched her, reaching out his left hand to her left shoulder.

Her eyes opened, the brilliance of the blue somehow deeper in the gray light of the room.

A smile tracked on her lips, her voice odd sounding. She whispered, "I love you," then closed her eyes.

John Rourke stood beside the bed for a time, watching her as she slept.

# Chapter 20

Sarah Rourke rammed the fresh thirty-round magazine into the M-16—for one of the thousands of times since she'd acquired the gun, she was grateful the previous owner (a brigand) had somehow gotten hold of the selective fire weapon. She pumped the trigger, making a professional three-round-burst—she was a professional by now, she realized. The nearest brigand biker fell back. But there were more coming.

The first attack in the early morning had waned quickly, and since then there had been sporadic gunfire from the other side of the field, but the distance too great. Then had come the second attack—a dead-on assault across the field. Her own weapon firing, Mary Mulliner firing the AR-15 and the hired hand—old Tim Beachwood—firing his own rifle—they had repelled the attack.

Beachwood was in the front of the house now, his rifle booming and audible over the roar of gunfire. "Michael!" Sarah shouted. "Go up and see if Tim needs anything—hurry but stay low."

"Right," the boy called out, then—as she looked back—he was gone. Annie, just six, sat under the heavy kitchen table, chairs stacked between the open wall side and herself just visible as Sarah looked for her. She was loading magazines for the Colt rifles. Her counting wasn't perfect yet, and as Sarah had fired through some of the magazines counting her shots with the bursts, she'd found magazines with thirty rounds, twenty-seven rounds, twenty-eight and even one that somehow the child had forced an extra round into—thirty-one.

Sarah pumped another burst, missing the brigand firing from the back of a fast moving pickup truck. "Annie—keep those magazines coming," Sarah called out.

"I'm hurrying, Mommie!"

"Good girl," Sarah called back. She was the unofficial leader—she realized that. Old Tim Beachwood had said it right after the shooting started. "I never fought no war," he'd said. "Too old for the last one—way too old for this one. But I hunted all my life—you point me the right winder and I'll start a killin'!"

She had shown him the right "winder" then. The gun—he had told her what it was—was something she'd already recognized. It was a lever action Winchester, the caliber .30-30. She had watched cowboy heroes using them in every Western film she'd ever seen.

Another brigand truck—the truck cut a sharp curve through the back yard, across Mary Mulliner's vegetable garden, a man in the truck bed waving—it wasn't a rifle, but a torch. Sarah snapped off a three-round burst, the man's body crumpling, the torch falling from his hands and to the ground, the body doubling forward and rolling off the truck bed, bouncing once as it hit the ground. Sarah tucked down, a stream of automatic weapons fire hammering through the shot out windows and into the cupboards on the far wall. "Stay down, Annie," Sarah screamed. She could hear the cups shattering in the cabinets, the glasses breaking.

"They mean to burn us," Mary Mulliner gasped, sucking in her breath audibly.

"Yes—they mean to burn us," Sarah nodded.

When this third attack had begun, Sarah had resigned

herself to the fact that there was no hope of victory. She had told Mary to shoot as little as possible. There had been three hundred and seventy-nine rounds of .223 ammo available when the battle had begun. There was less than half of that remaining, firepower the only means of holding the superior brigand numbers away from the house. Old Tim had had one hundred and three rounds of ammo for the .30-30. How much he had remaining she couldn't guess. There was an even hundred rounds of .45 ACP, only one pistol available to handle it—hers. She would save that until the rifle ammo was nearly gone, then use it to repel as many brigands as long as she could. She had decided—she would save at least four rounds—one for the Jenkins girl, hiding with Tim, helping him, Sarah hoped. One for Mary Mulliner. Two for her own children. She had seen what brigands could do to children—young boys, little girls. She had seen them do things to older women. She shivered—she had seen what they did to women like herself. Gang raped, left exhausted and dying by a roadside for the wild dogs to feast on.

She might save five rounds, she thought. She pumped the M-16's trigger. A three-round burst, then another and another. She shattered the windshield of the pickup truck coming dead-on for the back of the house. But the truck was still coming. A man stood up from the truck bed, a torch in his hands. He was swinging it.

Sarah pumped the M-16's trigger—the gun belched two rounds and was empty. The man fell back and the torch was gone from sight.

She sank behind the sink again as a burst of automatic weapons fire came.

This assault would end soon—she understood their tactics by now. Get the occupants to waste as much ammunition as possible. Dead men were apparently of no concern.

There would be another attack and another—then the

final rush.

She needed a tactic of her own.

"Tim—Tim!"

It was Michael's voice she heard.

"He's dead, Mommie—I think he's dead."

Sarah Rourke felt sick—her first thought was, "Who will replace him in the front of the house?"

"I can fire a gun—Daddy taught me a little."

She closed her eyes. "Take Mary's AR-15, Michael—and stay down."

She made the sign of the cross over her chest.

# Chapter 21

Michael Rourke sat by the window, Mary Mulliner beside him—he waited. He'd watched his mother do it many times before. He tried thinking about how it must feel.

"Michael—maybe you won't have to kill anybody."

"I killed a man once—maybe a second time. I'm not sure about that."

"But maybe—"

"It'll be all right. The stock for the rifle is too long for me so I can't hold it that well. But it'll be all right."

"You're only a little boy, Michael—"

"I'm eight years old."

"Michael—"

"It'll be all right, Aunt Mary," he told her.

He didn't know if it would be all right. His father had only just started teaching him to shoot seriously. He couldn't remember for certain, but he thought he was five the first time he'd been taken out into the woods behind the house and given a gun to shoot.

He remembered the gun—the Python. His father had cut his left hand holding the gun down in recoil. He remembered what he'd told his father, "Wow—that gun really kicks."

"It's a .357 Magnum," his father had said.

"Is that a powerful kind of gun?"

"Pretty powerful—you're going to have to be ten or

twelve before I let you try a .44—"

"I wanna try a .45—"

"Gotta be too careful with a .45—any automatic. Keep your fingers out of harm's way. Gotta be older." But he had let Michael try the CAR-15. And Michael had liked that, his father complaining, he remembered now, about the ammo cost, then laughing.

Michael reached out his right arm to its fullest extension—he could barely reach the trigger.

There was gunfire—coming from the rear of the house, but from outside.

He squinted his right eye, his left eye shut. He saw a man, coming out of the bushes at the front of the house.

"There's a man there," Mary Mulliner said. Her voice sounded upset to Michael.

"I know," he told her, trying to keep his own voice calm. He was afraid.

He pulled the trigger.

The recoil hurt his right shoulder and the top edge of the stock hit his jaw and that hurt.

But the man in the bushes fell over. Michael Rourke guessed the man was dead.

# Chapter 22

She had begun with three magazines—exactly full. She had fired out ten rounds from one of the magazines, firing on semi-automatic only now in order to conserve ammunition.

She assumed Michael had less than thirty rounds left.

There was the Winchester.

She picked it up, the unfamiliar shape in her hands seeming awkward to her.

She had watched old Tim load it.

Sarah Rourke, the M-16 leaning beside her against the sink cabinet, worked the lever—the hammer cocked.

She pushed herself up, a phalanx of brigand bikers rushing the house. She squeezed the trigger, the booming of the .30-30 deafening, her ears ringing, her shoulder aching—one brigand biker went down.

She worked the lever again as she ducked down.

"Mrs. Rourke—I'm afraid."

"So am I, Millie—don't worry," Sarah answered.

She could hear the little girl crying, hear Annie saying, "Mommie'll take care of us—everything'll be okay—you wait and see, Millie."

Sarah smiled in spite of herself—as Michael was becoming a man before her eyes, so was little Annie growing—but all to die. She bit her lower lip, raised herself up and fired, working the Winchester's lever, firing again, levering, firing again, levering and firing again.

Each shot had been a hit but the lever was too slow to work.

She dropped down, picking up the Colt rifle, her bare knees aching on the cold kitchen floor.

She pushed herself up, pumping the Colt's trigger at the phalanx of bikers. One shot, one dead. Another shot, another dead.

But they were still coming.

"Mommie!" It was Michael.

"The curtains are on fire!" It was Annie, Sarah feeling her heart in her mouth as she saw the girl standing up. And beyond Annie, into the living room—the parlor as Mary Mulliner called it—she could see flames.

"Michael—get out of there!" Sarah was on her feet, running, Michael standing up behind the sheet of flame, firing the AR-15 from the hip, Mary Mulliner crouched on the floor beside him, one dead brigand half through the window, the glass shattering out the rest of the way as Michael fired—two rounds, the body twitching twice, the man's clothes catching on fire.

The man was screaming.

Sarah fired the M-16, one round to the head. Mary Mulliner screamed, Sarah wheeling around, Annie and Millie running from the kitchen, Annie holding the .45.

"Mommie!"

Hands reached out from the kitchen doorway, a massive man in blue denim and black leather right behind them. Sarah fired the M-16, shifting the selector to full auto, the burst running from the man's bare sweating midsection and up along his chest in a ragged red line, the eyes wide open, the body lurching back through the doorway.

Sarah snatched the pistol from Annie's hands.

The other ammo—the Winchester. The spare magazines for the .45 and the M-16—all in the kitchen.

Another of the brigands was coming through the doorway, Sarah pushing the children down as the man raised a shotgun. Sarah fired, the M-16 coming up empty as the man fell back, the shotgun discharging into the chandelier in the center of the ceiling, Sarah hearing it, feeling the glass as it showered down on her.

"Mom!"

Michael's voice.

She wheeled, Michael firing his rifle, a man coming through the window, the curtains barely gone now as the fire spread to the outside wall, the smoke acrid.

Sarah started to jerk back the .45's hammer, but Michael was firing again, the body spinning out, the hands—bloodied—reaching for Michael's throat.

The boy rammed the rifle forward, the flash deflector punching into the center of the already floundering man's face.

The man fell back.

"My gun—it's empty, Mommie!"

"Get over here," Sarah shouted, drawing Annie and Millie against her skirt, holding the children with her left arm. Michael was beside her now, and so was Mary Mulliner.

The brigands would come—in a second, perhaps two—she would kill her children, kill Millie Jenkins, kill Mary Mulliner—she still didn't know if she could kill herself.

There were seven rounds in the pistol. Two for Michael and Annie. One for Millie. One for Mary. One for herself—five.

She had two left to fight.

The smoke was heavy now, the wind from outside the house that blew through the shot-out windows feeding the flames.

A brigand—she could see the look of lust in his eyes as he jumped through the window, the flames which caught at his shirt swatted out under his massive right hand.

She raised the .45.

"Get out of here!"

"Yeah—later," the man snarled, raising the rifle.

Sarah pulled the trigger. The .45 Government Model Colt bucked in her hand, the man's face registered shock, surprise. He toppled backward.

Michael had picked up a leg from a broken chair. She didn't know how it had gotten broken. He held it like a club.

"Let 'em come," he snarled.

"No," Sarah whispered.

One round was left. She edged back toward the stairwell, to escape the flames, to postpone—the inevitable.

"Mrs. Rourke!"

It was Millie Jenkins. Sarah looked down at her face, then at her eyes, then up the stairwell.

A man at the head of the stairs, a submachinegun in his hands.

Sarah pumped the trigger of the .45—once, then once again, the body lurching back, then doubling over, falling, the submachinegun spraying into the wall as Sarah pulled the children close to her.

The body fell at her feet, Mary Mulliner reaching down and picking up the submachinegun.

"It's empty I think," Mary almost hissed.

Sarah took the submachinegun—she thought it was an Uzi.

It was empty.

She looked at the dead man—no other gun, no spare magazines she could see.

There were not enough rounds left in the .45 for her to kill herself.

It had to be Michael first—he'd try to stop her otherwise.

She pressed the muzzle of the .45 to his head as she hugged him to her.

"I love you!" She screamed the words.

She started to squeeze the trigger.

"Mrs. Rourke!"

She looked to the doorway beyond the smoldering curtains, a man having gotten through. A young man, carrot red hair. "You're safe!"

It was Mary's son.

Calmly—Sarah raised the thumb safety on the .45 and handed the pistol to Mary Mulliner.

Every woman had the right, Sarah thought—at least once. She closed her eyes and fell, her head swimming, bright floaters in front of her eyes.

# Chapter 23

Sarah Rourke sat with her blue jeans across her lap, a blanket wrapped around her shoulders and her bare legs against the wind, the fire licking loudly in front of her.

"We got all your things out of the house—Mom told me where they were."

"How are the children, Bill?"

"Fine, Mrs. Rourke—Michael's sleeping and so's Annie. Millie's sitting on Mom's lap—but she's all right. Won't go to sleep though."

Sarah looked behind her at what had been the farmhouse. It was as burned and gutted as her own house in Georgia.

"I'm sorry for your mother's house," she whispered. "Sorry I fainted on you, too. But—"

"Hey—I understand it. I'm just a kid—at least I was. But—well, since the Night of The War, I seen a lot, ya know, ma'am."

"Yes—I know. I have too," Sarah told him. "Your resistance people were just like the cavalry—just in the nick of time," and she forced a laugh.

"Here," he said, sounding awkward to her. He handed her a gun—it was shiny. A .45, small like the ones her husband carried, but different somehow. "This was my Dad's—that's why Mom's crying. Not 'cause of the house, ya see—Dad—he didn't make it during the last raid on the Russians in Nashville."

She turned the gun over in her hands. As she looked at it, young Bill Mulliner continued talking to her. "Dad was a friend of this guy named Trapper—gunsmith up in Michigan before the Night of The War. Trapper made the gun up for him special. Started out a Colt Combat Commander—the one with the steel frame. Them's Smith & Wesson K-frame rear sights—gun's real short in the barrel and slide and the grip—a round shorter. Makes it nice to carry. And that's a Colt ambidextrous thumb safety on her—no grip safety—pinned in. That's a special nickel plating Trapper used."

"But this was your father's gun—you can't give it—"

"Ma'am—see, I got plenty a guns—and—well—if it weren't for you, my mom'd be dead too. Figure with this on ya, and a regular .45—you can use the same clips—"

"Magazines I think they're called," she smiled, feeling self-conscious at correcting a man about a gun.

"Yes'm—but you'll always have six extra rounds when ya need 'em. She's a smoothie of a shooter, ya know—and—well—so here," and he handed her a spare loaded magazine for the pistol.

She looked at the pistol in the firelight. The right side of the slide read "Trapper Gun" and there was a scorpion etched there in the metal, like there was on the flat black grips, barely visible in the flickering of the flames. "Thank you, Bill—I don't know what to say—I, ahh—"

"You just stay alive with it, ma'am—that's thanks enough and more."

"We can't stay here anymore, can we?" she said, still holding the gun, wrapping the blanket more tightly around her.

"No, ma'am—there's a big refugee camp not too far from here—should be safe from them brigand vermin. You and Mom and the children are gonna be okay there. Least ways ya should be."

She leaned across to the boy, still holding his dead

father's gun. She kissed the boy on the cheek.

"Mrs. Rourke," he drawled.

She leaned back against the side of the log that was being fed slowly into the fire, feeling the pleasant warmth. She closed her eyes. But she didn't let go of the pistol.

# Chapter 24

Colonel Nehemiah Rozhdestvenskiy picked up one of the rifles at random. There were dozens ranked along the wall, more still in crates. He personally liked the M-16—not as well as the Kalashnikov pattern rifles, but liked it nonetheless. And for the coming situation, American-made arms would be the best choice. He turned to the junior officer beside him—a Captain Revnik. "Captain—you must see to it that each of these rifles is thoroughly inspected. There is no use in storing arms which are defective. Any rifles which prove defective must be detail stripped and the defective part found, discarded or repaired and the rest of the parts binned according to type for use as spares."

"Yes, Comrade colonel," Revnik beamed. Rozhdestvenskiy disliked too much enthusiasm. "And the same with the pistols, Comrade colonel?"

"Yes—but only the .45 automatics—the Smith & Wesson revolvers will not be inventoried since there is no need to house .38 Special ammunition as well as .45. One standard pistol will suit our needs more than adequately. And of course each officer will have his own individual weapon." He patted the Colt Single Action Army under his uniform tunic.

"There must be adequate supplies for all needs, but most especially for the weapons—the individual weapons. For the five thousand M-16s we will need there must be five million rounds of 5.56mm military ball ammo—loaded in the eight hundred round steel containers will be best. These can then be sealed with wax as I've outlined in the master plans for the Womb. One million rounds of the .45 ACP ammunition for the one thousand pistols. This can be packed in greater bulk and likewise sealed. I'd suggest metal oil drums perhaps and the original boxes—again, all military ball ammunition.''

"Yes, Comrade colonel.''

Rozhdestvenskiy nodded, stepping away from the wall where the rifles leaned and toward the catwalk. He looked below him—men moving equipment—portable generators, arc lights. More men—crates being unloaded from large trucks onto smaller trucks which could be rolled directly aboard the waiting C-130s on the airfield two miles away.

"Work goes apace,'' he commented, leaning on the catwalk railing, swinging his body weight back and forth, feeling what he saw, feeling the power surging up in his blood. "But the pace must be quickened. If all the items are not secured in the Womb in a very, very short period of time, captain—all will have been for naught.''

"Yes, Comrade colonel—Comrade?''

"Yes, captain?''

"May I ask, Comrade colonel—why is this being—''

Rozhdestvenskiy felt his smile fade. "The survival of the race, Comrade—the survival of the race.''

Rozhdestvenskiy said no more.

# Chapter 25

Rourke, Paul Rubenstein and Natalia sat, their eyes transfixed as were the eyes of the submarine's complement not on duty—to the television monitors in the crew mess. It had been the same with San Francisco when they had passed the ruins—watching a city where once people lived now an underwater tomb. With this city it was doubly difficult—a young seaman first class had been born there, lived there—his mother, father, two sisters and wife and son had died there.

But he had insisted on watching—and now he wept.

Not one of the men touched him; Rourke, feeling perhaps like the rest of them, not knowing what to say, to do.

Natalia—wearing a robe borrowed from the captain, moving slowly, her left hand holding at her abdomen where Rourke had made the incisions—stood. Rourke started up after her, but she shook her head, murmuring, "No, John," then walked. She supported herself against the long, spotlessly clean tables, moving to alongside the weeping man.

"I am sorry—for your family—and for you," she whispered, Rourke watching her, watching all the others watching her.

The young man looked up. "Why'd you and your people wanna kill us—we coulda talked it out—or somethin'?"

"I don't know, sailor—I don't know," she whispered.
He looked at her, just shaking his head.

She moved her hands, touching them lightly to his shoulders. He looked down, his neck bent, his shoulders slumping. Natalia took a step toward him, leaning against him to help herself stand, her arms folding around his neck, his head coming to rest against her abdomen.

She closed her eyes as he wept.

Rourke breathed.

# Chapter 26

Rourke stood in the sail, the snowflakes thick and large, the temperature barely cold enough for them, he thought. They melted as they reached the backs of his hands on the rail, the knit cuffs of his brown leather bomber jacket, occasionally one of the larger flakes landing on his eyelashes—he would close his eyes for an instant and they would melt.

The flakes melted down from his hair, the melted snow running in tiny rivulets down his forehead and his cheeks—he could feel them.

Natalia Anastasia Tiemerovna shivered beside him and he folded his arm around her to give her warmth.

The submarine was moving—through the fjord-like cut in the land and toward the new coastline—it was north central California and beneath the wake the sub's prow cut were the bodies of the dead and cities they had lived in.

Rourke thought of this—he could not avoid thinking of it . . .

There was a bay that had been carved at the far end of the inlet, Commander Gundersen on the sail beside Rourke, Rubenstein and Natalia, in constant radio contact with his bridge for depth soundings of the fjord—it had been created by the megaquakes that had destroyed California beyond the San Andreas faultline on the Night of The War. There were no charts.

"I'm running even at eighteen feet below the waterline—shit," and Gundersen looked away from Rourke, snapping into the handset, "Wilkins—this is it—we get ourselves hung up—bad enough we can't dive. All stop, then give me the most accurate soundings you can all through the bay—wanna channel I can stay over where I can dive if I have to. Once you've got that, feed in the coordinates and back her up—you got the con."

"Aye, captain," the voice rattled back.

Gundersen put down the set. "You've been avoiding Captain Cole."

Rourke nodded, saying, "You didn't want a fight on board ship."

"Well—the time has come, hasn't it—let's all get below and talk this out so we know what the hell we're doing, huh?" Gundersen didn't wait for an answer, but retrieved the handset, depressing the push-to-talk button. "Wilkins—Gundersen. Get that Captain Cole sent over to my cabin in about three minutes."

"He was just up here looking for you, skipper."

"Terrific—well—tell him I'm looking for him."

Gundersen started below, cautioning. "Watch your step, miss," to Natalia. She nodded, starting down the hatchway after him.

Rubenstein caught at Rourke's arm. "We really gonna go through with this?"

"Cole wants those warheads—whether it's just carrying out his orders or for some other reason. Only way we can know is to be there with him when he gets them."

"I was afraid you were gonna say that."

Rourke felt himself smile. "Come on—watch your step. Slippery."

Rubenstein nodded as Rourke looked away—there was more to watch your step about than ice on the sail, Rourke thought.

# Chapter 27

The weather had turned cold again—spring was gone. She wondered if it were forever.

The refugee camp a short distance away had been eight days away. She stood now on a low rise, seeing it in the distance. Eight days—large Soviet forces moving into factory towns along the way, brigand concentrations—days of waiting in caves and in the woods—days of rain, of cold.

She shivered, reaching her hands up to tug at the bandanna that covered her hair, to pull it lower over her ears. She folded her arms around herself, hugging herself—but the cold would not go away.

"We can rest here," the gruff-voiced resistance leader announced. Gruff-voiced, she thought, but a warm man, a good man. Pete Critchfield, Bill Mulliner's father's second in command and now the leader by default. But he seemed a good leader, she thought.

She looked behind her—Annie and Millie Jenkins rode the mule, Michael walked beside.

"Stop for a while," she breathed—"the camp's in sight, but a little distance yet."

They were in a field of jagged, carelessly arranged rocks on the rise, mists covering much of the valley, the fine mist coming down on them as well on the rise.

The mule's hide smelled as she took Annie into her arms and helped her to the ground.

Michael held the mule's halter. Sarah helped Millie down.

"You kids get under some shelter—got a shelter half goin' up," Bill Mulliner ordered.

Michael looked at him, saying nothing, then nodded and took the two girls in tow.

Sarah shifted the weight of her knapsack, tossing it to the ground near the rocks and then unslinging the M-16 from her right shoulder.

"Mrs. Rourke—there's shelter for you, too," Pete Critchfield said, passing her. He was always moving, always doing something—never standing still.

"I'm all right here, Mr. Critchfield," she called after him, not knowing if he'd heard or not.

She sat on the rock nearest her, feeling the cold and dampness as it worked through her blue jeans to her panties and then to her skin.

"Here, ma'am," and Bill Mulliner handed her a blanket. "Sit on this."

She smiled up at him, took the blanket and placed it under her. The blanket was damp feeling, but at least not so cold as the rock. "The weather's crazy, isn't it?" she said, just for conversation.

Bill Mulliner sat down beside her and she rearranged the blanket which brought him quite close to her, but at least made the young man more comfortable. "Them sunsets—so red. The thunder all the time in the sky—spooky to me," he nodded, lighting his pipe. He looked silly smoking it, but she wasn't about to tell him that.

"Maybe it's the end—for all of us," she said after a moment.

"Way I see it—well, folks used to talk in the magazines and books and on the television how's a nuclear war would kill ever'body. But ever'body ain't dead," and he looked at her.

"Maybe you're right," she answered, her voice low.

She shifted the pistol belt she now wore—inherited from one of the dead brigands at the Mulliner farm. The .45, her husband's gun—was on the belt in a flap covered black leather holster with "US" stamped into the flap. She had canvas magazine holders on the belt as well—six extra magazines for the .45. The smaller gun—the Trapper Scorpion .45—was in a homemade belt holster—same holster Bill Mulliner's father had used, on a belt threaded through the belt loops of her jeans under her coat. It was a good way to carry a gun, she decided—it was always on her, except when she slept, and beside her then when she did.

She unlatched the web material pistol belt, wrapped the belt around the flap holster and set the big .45 on the ground beside her—she was tired.

"Things'll be fine once you and your family reach the refugee camp—people there'll help ya out—and people there for you to help too, ma'am. Lots a sick people. Lots of people who lost their families and all. But it's a good place—church service twice a week—Wednesday nights and Sunday mornin's—preacher'd do more, but he keeps up goin' out the rest of the time lookin' for more sick people to bring in. Good man, the preacher. Methodist—me, I'm Baptist, but that's all right."

"I guess we were Presbyterian before the War—didn't go much to church," she told him.

"Me—heck, ma'am—I miss church. We had a youth group—I woulda been out of it the next year anyways—And the Scouts—my Scout troop was through the church—Pastor was my scout leader from the time I first got out of my Cub pack 'til I made Eagle Scout."

"Your parents must have been very proud of you—I know your mother still is," Sarah whispered.

"I liked that life—don't spose we'll ever have that life again."

"Did you have a girl?" she asked him, then felt sorry

for asking as she watched his eyes.

"Yes, ma'am," he answered after a moment, sighing hard and loud. "Yes, ma'am—I had a girl. Pretty hair like yours—long like yours is."

Sarah felt he wanted her to ask—so she did. "What happened to your girl, Bill?"

The boy licked his lips, looked at her and then looked away, knocking out the pipe against the heel of his workboot. "Dead, ma'am. What got me in the Resistance. She lived in town, ya know—some of them brigand trash came through right after it all happened. I—ahh—I found her—they'd, ahh—" He didn't finish it.

Sarah reached out to him, putting her left arm across his shoulders, her left hand touching his neck as he leaned forward, not looking at her.

"They'd—they'd raped her—real bad—real—it was—the stuff—all over her legs and her belly and her face—it—it was all beat up. She just died I guess—right in the middle of it all—her name was Mary—like my mom's—" He started to cry and Sarah leaned close to him. There wasn't anything she could say.

# Chapter 28

"I need Doctor Rourke with me—Rubenstein can stay here. And no guns for Rourke," Cole said flatly.

Gundersen wove the fingers of his hands together. "I anticipated that, Captain Cole. I've talked briefly here with Doctor Rourke. Sending a man out unarmed into what might be out there would be like committing murder. Doctor Rouke gets his guns—"

"I object to that, sir!"

"I'll note that objection in my log," Gundersen went on placidly. Rourke watched his eyes. "And as to Mr. Rubenstein—if he chooses to accompany his friend, he certainly may. If you like, Lieutenant O'Neal—he's my missile officer and hasn't had much to do since we fired all our missiles you know—well, he's coming along as well as are a few of my men—a landing party. Lieutenant O'Neal can be responsible for Mr. Rubenstein if that suits you better. And as to Major Tiemerovna—there's no policy decision to be made there. She's not strong enough yet to travel. So she doesn't need her guns. Questions about that, captain?"

"I still protest, sir—once we're on land, this mission is mine."

"But this mission involves my submarine, mister—and getting those missile warheads safely on board this boat directly affects the safety of my crew. So some of my people go along, like it or not."

"I want to send out a recon patrol right away—before the shore party."

"A wise move—I'll let you handle that. If you'd like any of my men to acc—"

"No—no, sir. My men can handle that. That's what they're trained for."

"Can I say something?" Rourke asked.

"Certainly, Doctor Rourke," Gundersen nodded.

Rourke saw Natalia, Paul—even Cole staring at him. "That recon party could be a mistake—we can recon as we go. We have to go from here anyway, regardless of what's out there. Only way to reach Filmore Air Force Base. Sending out a patrol from here will only serve to alert any potentially hostile force to our intentions of going inland. I say we move out under cover of darkness—get ourselves well inland before dawn and go from there."

"Bullshit, Rourke!"

"There's a lady present, mister," Gundersen snapped. "And I agree with Doctor Rourke."

"The land portion of the mission is mine—I intend to send a recon patrol out now—I've got men geared up and ready."

Rourke shrugged.

Rubenstein cleared his throat, Rourke watching as the younger man pushed his glasses up off the bridge of his nose. "John's right—we let anybody out there know what we're up to, all they're going to do is set a trap for us."

"If this meeting is about over, commander—I've got a final briefing for my men."

Rourke lit one of his cigars, looking at Cole, studying him. "You leading it—the recon patrol, I mean?"

"Corporal Henderson—"

"Ohh—well, I don't care much if he ever comes back anyway. How's his face doing?" Henderson was the man Rourke had put away for shooting Natalia.

Cole glared at Rourke, saying, "One of these days, Doctor Rourke—after we contact Colonel Teal, after we secure those warheads—it's you and me."

Rourke nodded. "It scares me just to think about it," and he exhaled the gray smoke from his lungs.

# Chapter 29

The faces—she watched them as they watched her. She held Michael's right hand in her left, the boy saying nothing, but watching the faces, too.

Sarah shifted the weight of her M-16, the rifle carried now cross body on its sling, her right fist balled around the pistol grip. She had not seen so many people in one place—crowded together in one place—since before the Night of The War. It mildly frightened her. She had seen other large groups—but she didn't count them people. The brigands—they were less than animals. The Russians—she refused to think of them any more than she had to. But she thought every once in a while of the Soviet major—the man she had met during the resistance escape in Savannah, whom she had met once again in Tennessee.

He had spared her.

She had watched his eyes, seeing something there she had seen in her husband's eyes. And she wondered what he had seen in her eyes.

She shook her head.

"What's wrong, Momma?" Michael looked up at her—he was nearly to the height of her breasts when he stood erect.

"Nothing—just all these people—" She stopped, Pete Crichfield having stopped, even Bill Mulliner's golden retriever, the dog the children had constantly played with at the farm, having stopped.

Bill Mulliner came up beside her. "That fella on the porch—David Balfry—he's the commander."

"The commander?"

"Yeah—college professor before the Night of The War—he's sort of the headman for the resistance in Tennessee here."

She looked beyond Pete Critchfield's massive shoulders. "David Balfry," she repeated.

He was her own age, she judged. Tall, straight, lean-featured. Close cropped blond hair, a smile lighting his face for an instant.

"Mrs. Rourke!" It was Pete Critchfield, calling to her.

"Yes, Mr. Critchfield."

"You and your boy come up here and meet David." Sarah left the ragged column, walking closer to the knot of people, still watching her—watching all of the new-comers, she told herself. There were wounds—bandaged, some not cleanly. There were missing limbs, eyes—terrible burns on the faces and exposed hands of some of the people in the crowd. She pushed past, stopping at the porch steps of the farmhouse.

"Mrs. Rourke—I heard of your work in Savannah with the resistance there. It's an honor to meet you," and David Balfry extended his hand. The fingers were long, like the fingers of a pianist or violinist were supposed to be but so rarely were.

She felt his hand press around hers.

She looked into his eyes—they were green. They were warm.

"It's—it's a pleasure to meet you, too—Mr. Balfry."

"It used to be Professor Balfry—now it's just David. Sarah—isn't it?"

"Yes," she told him. She wondered quickly what else he would ask her.

"May I call you Sarah?"

She nodded, saying nothing.

"I understand your husband was a doctor—"

"Is a doctor," she told him, shifting her feet in her tennis shoes.

"Yes—but were you ever a nurse—"

"Not really—but I've done a lot of it."

"Reverend Steel—I think he could use some help with the sick—after you settle in, of course."

"Of course—I mean—yes. I'll help," she told him.

Balfry extended his right hand again, this time to Michael's head, tousling his hair. She felt the boy's right hand tensing in her left, saw him step away.

David Balfry smiled. "We'll get to know each other, son," and he turned to Pete Critchfield. Sarah felt awkward just standing there, but didn't know what else to do.

Michael tugged at her hand.

Something else tugged at her as well.

Balfry looked away from Pete Critchfield once and she thought he smiled at her.

# Chapter 30

The landing party had not returned. Rourke, Cole, Gundersen, Lieutenant O'Neal and Paul Rubenstein stood in the sail, watching the dark shore. There was no moonlight, the sky overcast still and the incredibly large flakes of snow still falling, but the temperature still almost warm.

Rourke glanced at the luminous black face of the Rolex on his left wrist, cupping his right hand over it to make the darkness deep enough that the numerals would glow.

"They've been gone for eight hours—supposed to be back two hours ago. If they were my men, Captain Cole, I think I might go looking for them."

"Yeah—well—"

"Yeah—well," Rourke mimicked. He shifted his shoulder under the bomber jacket, the familiar weight of the Detonics pistols there in the double Alessi rig something he was glad to have back again. The Sparks Six Pack rode his trouser belt, the magazines freshly loaded and the ammo from each all hand cycled through his pistols to assure the magazines functioned properly—they did. These six magazines plus the magazines he normally carried, vastly increased his ready firepower. Rubenstein stood beside him, the Browning coming into his hands. He hand cycled the slide, chambering a round off the top of the magazine, then made the 9mm pistol disappear under his Army field jacket.

"Ready when you are, John," Paul smiled.

"Captain—" It was Lieutenant O'Neal, the missile officer. "Sir, I can get together part of that shore party right now—"

Rourke interrupted him. "Belay that—that's what you say in the Navy, isn't it?"

O'Neal's normally red cheeks flushed as he laughed. "That's right, sir."

"I've got a better idea, I think—if Commander Gundersen approves," Rourke added. "Cole, Paul, myself—those three other troopers of Captain Cole's—we go in now. Hit the beach in a rubber boat if you got one, then get up into those rocks. If that recon patrol Hendersen led got nailed, it was probably pretty soon after they hit shore. You save that landing party if we're not back by dawn—and have 'em ready in case we come back sooner with somebody chasing us."

"That sounds good to me," Gundersen nodded. "Captain Cole?" Gundersen raised his eyebrows, as if waiting for Cole to respond.

"No other choice, I guess," Cole nodded.

"I'll get the rest of the gear," Rubenstein said, disappearing toward the hatchway leading down from the sail.

"And with your permission, sir," O'Neal volunteered to Gundersen. "I'll get that inflatable geared up."

"You got it," Gundersen nodded.

Rourke stared past Gundersen—the shore was a darker gray line against the near blackness of the water, and in the distance above the rocks which marked the coast was a lighter gray—it was the sky. The water in the inlet was calm—the deck on the sail almost motionless under him.

There were people in the darkness—and Rourke didn't doubt that someone of them at least was watching him from the rocks.

As it always was—despite the elements, the forces of nature—the true danger was man.

# Chapter 31

The waves made a soft, almost rhythmical slapping sound against the gunwales of the gray inflatable boat; Rourke crouched in the prow, the CAR-15 ready, Rubenstein beside him, Cole and his three troopers filling out the center and aft section, two of the three troopers rowing.

There had always been considerable talk about a sixth sense, but nothing concretely proven, at least as far as Rourke considered it. But if there were a sixth sense—and gut feelings had convinced him long ago there were—he felt its activation now.

"I feel something," Rubenstein murmured beside him.

Rourke smiled, saying nothing. Beneath the bomber jacket against the cold, he wore a dark blue crew neck sweater from the submarine's stores—but he still shivered. It wasn't the cold doing it.

There was a whitish outline gleaming ahead—the shoreline where the waves lapped against it now. The tide was high, and this cut the distance to the rocks beyond the beach.

"Kill those oars," Rourke commanded, stripping away his leather gloves, stuffing them into one of the bomber jacket's outside patch pockets, then dipping his hands into the water on both sides of the prow. "Use your hands," he rasped, his fingers numbing from the water temperature already—but there was no choice.

It took several minutes of the slow movement, barely

able to fight the waves rolling back from the shore, to move with the tide and reach the land. Rourke throwing a leg out, water splashing up over the collar of his combat boot, then his other leg out, Rubenstein into the water too now. The surf splashed against the prow of the boat, turning into a fine, icy spray, Rourke flexing his fingers against the fabric of the boat as he hauled at it, snow still coming down—no more heavily than before, but no less heavily either.

"Come on, Paul," he rasped to the younger man, then to Cole, "Get your butts outa the boat and give us a hand! Come on!"

Cole sprang from the boat, dousing himself in the water, his three men following suit but with less lack of grace. Water dripping from him, Cole reemerged, cursing—

"Shut up, damnit!" Rourke snapped. The boat was nearly up from the surf, Rourke glancing to Paul, saying, "Together," then hauling at the rubber boat, over the last roll of breakers, both men heaving together, the boat onto the sand.

"You and you—you help 'em," Rourke rasped to the three soldiers. "Get the boat out of here—back in those rocks. Secure it in case the tide does get higher."

Rourke swung the CAR-15 off his shoulder where it had hung muzzle down. He pulled the rubber plug from the muzzle and dropped it into his musette bag where he carried some of his spare magazines and other gear. He shifted the rifle forward, working the bolt and chambering the top cartridge out of the freshly loaded thirty-round stick.

He started forward across the sand, feeling he was being watched, waiting for it to come—

It came.

"Kill them!"

The shout—somehow oddly not quite human.

Rourke wheeled, snapping the CAR-15's muzzle forward, ramming the flash deflector into the face of the man—man?—coming for him. The machete dropped from the right hand as the body reeled.

"No guns unless we have to," Rourke half shouted, flicking the safety on for the CAR-15. He stepped toward the attacker, the man starting to move, a revolver rising in his right hand, already the sounds of more of the attackers going for Rubenstein and the others coming to him over the sound of the waves, over the whistling of the wind. Rourke's right foot snaked out, cross body, catching the man's gunhand wrist, the revolver sailing off into the darkness.

Rourke let the rifle slide out of the way on its sling, his left foot coming up, going for the man's jaw. He missed, the body rolling across the sand, coming upright. There was another knife, smaller than the machete, but not by much.

Rourke grabbed for the AG Russell Sting IA in his trouser band, the small knife coming into his palm, the black skeletonized blade shifting outward in his left hand as the man—he wore a motley collection of clothing and animal skins—made his lunge. Rourke sidestepped, the man steaming past him, Rourke's knife hammering down, the blade biting into flesh somewhere over the right kidney, the body's momentum tearing the blade through and down, Rourke's left wrist hurting badly, the knife slipping from his grip.

He turned, hearing something—feeling something. Two men—like the first, half in the clothing of "civilized" men and half in animal skins, unshaven, hair wildly blowing in the wind. One had a long bladed knife secured, lashed to a pole—a primitive pike or spear. The second held a pistol.

Rourke violated his own rule; not bothering with the CAR-15, not having the time to get at it, snatching at the

Detonics under his left armpit, his right fist closing on the black rubber Pachmayr gripped butt, his right thumb jacking back the hammer, his first finger into the trigger guard as the pistol came on line, twitching against the trigger, the gleaming stainless handgun bucking in his hand, the man with the pistol taking the impact somewhere near the center of mass, the 185-grain JHP throwing him back into the sand.

The one with the improvised pike was swinging it, the blade making a whooshing sound as it cut the air. Rourke edged back, hearing more gunfire now from the beach—the light rattle of Paul's Schmeisser, lighter than the shotgun blast he heard following it.

Rourke edged back, the pike coming again, Rourke dropping to his right knee, scissoring out his left leg for a sweep as the man followed up on his lunge, the blade inches above Rourke's head, Rourke's left leg connecting behind the right knee of the man with the pike. The body started shifting forward, like a deadfall tree in the wind.

Rourke rolled left, pulling his right leg after him, the body slapping down against the sand, a shout issuing from the man. "Kill them! Kill the heathens!"

"Heathens," Rourke muttered, rolling again, getting to his feet.

The man was starting up, his pike coming up, Rourke feigning a kick with his right, half wheeling, snapping out his left combat-booted foot. His leg took the shock, his left knee aching as the toe of his boot impacted against the right side of the man's face.

Rourke wheeled, two more of the wildmen coming for him. He dodged left, one of the men—a machete in his right hand—bringing the blade down hard through the air, barely missing Rourke's right arm.

Rourke pumped the Detonics, nailing the second man, this one with a gun.

He wheeled, the sound of the machete in the air again

113

making him do it. The blade arced past his nose, the man's arm at maximum extension. "That's never a good idea," Rourke cautioned him, wheeling half left, snapping his right leg out in a double kick to the man's face, the man falling backward.

Rourke started down the beach, Rubenstein locked in combat with a man twice his size, Rubenstein's pistol high in the air, over his head, the wildman fighting him holding it there. Suddenly, the wildman doubled forward, Rubenstein half stepping away, rubbing momentarily at his right knee, then pushing the Browning High Power forward, the man starting to rise, both hands clasped to his crotch. The muzzle flash against the darkness of the sky, the rocks and the water were brilliant for an instant, the high pitched pop of the 9mm almost lost in the wind and the noise of the surf, then drowned in the scream of the wildman as he spun out, both hands going to his neck. He fell. Rubenstein turned, backing off from a second man, Rourke starting toward him. The second man had no weapon Rourke could see. He swung his right fist, a classic barroom brawl haymaker. Rubenstein blocked it neatly with his left forearm, stepped into the man's guard and launched his right fist forward, the man's head snapping back, Rubenstein's left crashing down across the exposed jaw, the body sagging down to the knees. Rubenstein's right knee smashed forward, against the tip of the jaw, the wildman's head snapping back again—there was an audible snapping sound. The body sagged down, lurching forward, still kneeling, not moving—dead, Rourke judged.

"Come on, Paul!"

Rourke started toward Cole and his men, the four battling twice that many of the wildmen.

Rourke slipped the CAR-15 forward, the safety going off under his right thumb, then the stock telescoping under his hand.

114

The nearest of the wildmen turned from Cole and the others, starting for him. Rourke was shifting the sling off from his left shoulder. There wasn't time to finish it. His right foot snapped out, catching the man's crotch, the wildmen screaming but not stopping. Rourke wheeled three hundred sixty degrees, free of the sling now.

As the wildman spun toward him, he arched the butt of the CAR-15 up, the heel of the flat metal buttplate catching at the tip of the wildman's jaw, the head snapping back, Rourke smashing out with the full flat of the butt for the center of the man's face.

Rourke wheeled half right as the body dropped away, tucking down his right elbow to recover the stroke, slashing down with the muzzle of the CAR as if there had been a bayonet in place. The flash deflector laid open the right cheek of the man coming at him with the machete. Rourke snapped his left foot out, going into a forward thrust, the flash deflectored muzzle punching into the attacker's Adam's apple. The man went down.

Rourke took the step forward on his right, pivoting, the bayonetless rifle in a high guard position, a wildman with a spear rushing him. Rourke swatted the spear away, taking a long stride out with his right leg, dipping low, snapping the butt of the rifle up in an arc, the toe of the butt impacting against the left cheekbone of the man with the spear, the body falling back as Rubenstein stepped in from the far right, the pistol grip of the Schmeisser connecting against the man's left temple.

Rourke wheeled, sidestepping as Rubenstein advanced on two of the wildmen, one armed with a riot shotgun, another with an assault rifle. Rubenstein's MP-40 was already spitting, Rourke snatching the Detonics from his belt, thumbing down the safety and emptying the pistol's remaining four rounds into the two men.

Rubenstein started forward, Rourke reaching out the right hand which still held the empty Detonics, the slide locked back over the spent magazine.

"Wait!"

Cole was the only one still fighting—a wildman roughly his own size, blond shoulder length hair falling across his face and half obscuring the irregular beard.

The man was barehanded—so was Cole, his rifle gone somewhere, the .45 he'd threatened Rourke with still in his holster.

The wildman's hands reached out, Rourke not shifting his eyes as by feel he swapped for a fresh magazine in the Detonics, leaving the six pack intact, getting one from his musette bag.

By feel again, he found the slide stop, thumbing it down, hearing the slide rake forward.

Cole had the .45 out of the holster now, the man he fought swatting it away, the pistol discharging skyward. Cole slumped back, making to fire the .45 again as the blond haired wildman came at him. Nothing happened.

Rourke pumped the Detonics' trigger once, the wild-man's head exploding on the left side, the body sprawling back across the sand.

Cole was looking up, at Rourke, then down to his gun. Rourke took four steps forward and stopped beside Cole. He reached down, carefully taking the pistol. The slide was only part way into battery, the full metal case 230-grain hardball round somehow jammed diagonally, bullet pointing upward.

"Odd," Rourke almost wispered. "Jam like that in a military gun. Wouldn't have happened though if you'd fed that round into the chamber off the top of the magazine." Rourke thumbed the magazine catch release, pulling the magazine out, the half chambered round jamming it. He counted the glimmers of brass in the witness holes, the bottom hole empty only. He jacked back the slide, popping the seventh round out of the breech and into the palm of his right hand. "Like I told you." He flashed what he hoped was his biggest smile as he tossed Cole the empty pistol, the magazine and the loose round.

Rourke turned away, under his breath muttering, "Shit—"

# Chapter 32

Sarah kept her eyes closed. She could hear Michael breathing, hear Annie snoring a little as she always did. She heard nothing from Millie but had checked a few moments earlier—the girl had always been a sound, unimaginative sleeper.

She was alone in the small tent except for them—except for her thoughts. She kept her eyes closed tight, but could not sleep.

There had been no word through Bill Mulliner—no word of John. She had asked David Balfry and he had promised to put out feelers that very night—to see if her husband had contacted the resistance or if U.S. II knew his whereabouts.

"David Balfry," she murmured.

He was a handsome man, by any woman's standards, she thought.

She wondered why he had smiled at her.

She rolled over, the blankets on the hard, damp ground not so uncomfortable she couldn't sleep—since the Night of The War she had slept under far worse conditions.

She made herself think of the refugees—in the morning, Reverend Steel would be back and she'd begin helping him as a nurse—

She couldn't stay forever at the refugee center.

She would take up the search for John if no news came of his whereabouts. She would do that.

John was strong—David Balfry—he was strong, too. She remembered the way his hand had felt. It had been a long time since a man had held her hand like that, no matter how brief.

She closed her eyes tighter, rolling onto her back again. She mentally reconstructed her husband's features. His eyes—they could see through you, she remembered. His forehead was high, but it had always been high, his hair thick, healthy, dark. There had been gray hair on his chest—prematurely gray, she had realized then and told herself now. She thought of the hardness of his muscles when he held her in his arms.

She opened her eyes, staring up at the tent beyond the hazy darkness, the grayness.

"John," she whispered, barely hearing her own words, feeling them more. "I need you now—" She realized what her hands were doing—and she kept them there, closing her eyes.

# Chapter 33

Rourke understood it now—why no one had come in response to the shots.

The chanting and screaming would have drowned out any noise.

The wildmen chanted, men and women, dressed in the same curious mixture of tattered conventional clothing, animal skins and rags.

The shore party Cole had risked did the screaming. Men—all of them hung on crudely made crosses of limbs and scrap timbers—were being tortured in a variety of ways. Pyres were set about the bases of each cross and Rourke watched now as one of the wildmen reached a faggot into the bonfire which crackled loudly in the wind in the center of the ring of crosses, the ring of crucified men and their torturers.

The faggot glowed and sparked in the wind—it was now a torch.

"Holy shit," Rubenstein murmured, Rourke feeling the younger man's breath beside him.

"You might say that," Rourke observed.

"What are we gonna do?" It was Cole's voice, his whisper like a blade being drawn across a rough stone.

"That's an odd question for you to ask me," Rourke noted, not looking at Cole, watching the progress instead of the wildmen who held the torch. "We left one man dead on the beach—well, that isn't really true. We sent his body back with the other two and the two prisoners. And one of your two men was wounded. Now even if Lieutenant O'Neal had his shore party in the boats, should still be ten minutes before they'd even hit the beach. Then another fifteen minutes' climb up here. I'd say that leaves only the three of us."

"The three of us against them," Cole snarled. "You're crazy—there must be a hundred of 'em—all of 'em with guns and more of those damn knives."

Rourke turned and looked at Cole, then at Paul Rubenstein. "I guess that doesn't leave three of us then—only leaves two of us. You guard the rear, Cole—your rear. Looks like you're pretty damned experienced at it anyway."

Rourke pushed himself up over the rocks, feeling Cole tug at him. He looked back at the man.

He didn't have to say anything. Paul whispered, "What he meant was—save your ass—seems you got a lot of practice at it."

Rourke finished moving across the rocks, hearing Rubenstein beside him as he slipped down onto the grassy expanse below, hiding in the shadow there while he watched the man with the torch stop in front of one of the crosses. "Ohh, boy," he whispered to himself.

# Chapter 34

Rourke's left hand snaked out through the darkness, in his right the A.G. Russell black chrome Sting IA he'd retrieved from the dead body on the beach. The left hand grasped a handful of hair, jerking the head under it back, the right hand plunging the knife down into the voicebox to stifle any scream. He pulled the knife, then raked it once ear to ear as the body fell back toward him—just in case.

He'd killed the man to avoid having someone directly at his back.

He stepped out of the shadow of the trees now and into the meager glow of the fire, some hundred yards away still from the ring of crosses.

The wildman who held the torch stood beneath the cross of one of the shore party—Rourke thought vaguely—at the angle he wasn't able to be sure—that it was Corporal Henderson.

It stood to reason—make an example of the leader and burn him first.

Considering what Henderson had done, Rourke had at least a twinge of desire to let the man die. But that wasn't his way—and he knew it wasn't.

Rourke glanced at the Rolex as he rolled back the cuff of the bomber jacket and the sweater beneath it. It had been five minutes—time enough for Paul to be in position on the far side of the ring of crosses. He discounted any help from Cole completely.

It was time.

Rourke started forward, searching his pockets for the Zippo lighter which bore his initials, finding it, lighting the chewed stump of dark tobacco in the left corner of his mouth.

He put the light away, swinging the CAR-15 forward. While he'd been up in the rocks, he'd reloaded the spent and partially spent Detonics magazines. Counting the six pack, he had twelve magazines, including the two in the guns—seventy-two rounds. He carried six spare magazines for the CAR-15, plus the one already up the well—no loose ammo for these. The Python was at his right hip, 158-grain JHPs loaded, three speedloaders ready, plus the loose ammo in the dump pouches on his belt.

If it took him one shot per man—and woman— around the crosses and they all stood perfectly still while he shot so there would be no chance of a miss, he'd have plenty of ammo to spare.

Rourke smiled to himself—somehow, he doubted things would work that way.

The CAR-15 slung cross body under his right arm, he stopped walking, less than twenty-five yards from the nearest cross—the one on which Henderson was hung, the one before which the wildman stood holding the torch.

Rourke balanced the rifle butt against his right hip, pulling the trigger once, firing into the air.

The chanting stopped, the screaming didn't.

The faces of the wildmen and their women turned— toward him.

His voice little above a whisper, Rourke rasped, "You can stop all this or you're dead—your play, guys."

That was something else he doubted would work that way.

# Chapter 35

"Kill the heathen!"

The man with the torch shouted it, Rourke already lowering the muzzle of the CAR-15, his trigger finger moving once, gutshooting the man where he stood.

The screaming was louder now, drowning out the screams of the crucifixion victims—but the cries from the wildmen and their women—"Kill the heathen!"

Rourke had the CAR-15 to hip level now, pumping the trigger in rapid, two-shot semi-automatic bursts. Men and women ran everywhere, screaming, some running toward him, some running blindly like trapped animals. He could hear small arms fire from the far side of the ring of crosses—Rubenstein, he hoped.

As a wedge in the wildmen opened he could see something more immediate. The wildman he'd gut shot had somehow crawled toward the pyre beneath the cross on which Henderson was hung—and the pyre was beginning to burn.

He started to run, toward the cross, the flames licking higher, fanned it seemed by their own heat, higher pitched than the screams and curses and threats of the wildmen the scream from Henderson—Rourke could see the man's face, orange lit and shadowed, as the flames seemed sucked up toward his flesh.

"Help me!"

Rourke spun half left, pumping the CAR-15's trigger

again, putting down a man rushing him with a machete. He pumped the CAR-15 again, a woman with a revolver. Red flowers of blood blossomed on her chest as she stumbled back.

Hands reached for him, Rourke sidestepping, a bear-sized man grasping at him.

No time to shoot, no way to swing the CAR-15's muzzle on line, Rourke hammered out hard to his right with the rifle's butt, doubling the man forward. Rourke's right knee smashed upward, catching the face midway between the lips and the base of the nose, blood spurting as the shout issued from the mouth that now looked like a raw wound.

Rourke swung the CAR-15 forward, still counting his shots, firing rapid two-shot bursts into the running, screaming men and women around him. He was ten yards from the cross now, changing sticks for the CAR, Henderson's screams beyond what could have come from a human, Rourke thought. The flames were licking at the skin of his bare legs, the words Henderson screamed unintelligible save for the agony they expressed.

Rourke slammed the fresh magazine home, working the bolt, turning as three men and a woman rushed him. He pumped the CAR-15's trigger, nailing the nearest of the four, then pumped the trigger again, getting the woman.

The two men came at him in a low rush, Rourke losing his balance as he pumped the trigger, shooting one of the men in the chest, the body rolling away. The second man's hands were on his throat, Rourke stumbling back, hitting the ground hard, the flames there scorchingly hot on his hands, his neck.

The fingers were closing tightly on him—floaters were crossing his eyes, gold, yellow, green.

Rourke's left hand found the butt of the Sting IA, his fingers jerking it free of the leather. He began stabbing it, into the strangler's right side. In—out. In—out. In—out.

The grip seemed only to tighten, the colors of the floaters going lighter, unconsciousness coming, his right arm pinned in the sling and useless.

Rourke smashed up with his right knee, feeling it strike the hardness of bone rather than the crushing softness of testicles.

The knife. It was out, his left arm going limp.

He spun his arm downward like a pendulum, feeling the blade bite deep, the stickiness of blood spurt covering his left hand, the weight of the man above him beginning to sag, the grip in the fingers not loosening.

He wrenched the knife free, then using the last strength he had, hammered it downward, contacting the tip of the spearpoint, pear-shaped blade against the bare upper arm, blood gushing as the skin ripped while Rourke dragged the knife down and along the arm's length.

The grip on his neck eased.

He smashed his right knee upward again, hammering with it in short jabs, searching for the testicles—there was a scream, the first sound the man had made—Rourke felt the squish of flesh against his knee.

The grip on his neck loosened completely, Rourke jabbing the knife in again, into the chest, the body lurching back.

Rourke rolled onto his stomach, coughing, gasping for breath, his right arm numb.

His left hand, sticky with the blood, snaked toward the Detonics pistol under his right armpit, found the rubber grip, wrenched the pistol through the speedbreak through the trigger guard and out of the leather, the thumb slipping against the small spurred hammer because of the wetness of the blood. The man was up, hurtling himself forward, the knife still impaled in the right side of his chest, the right arm covered in blood.

Rourke's right thumb swiped again at the hammer, the hammer coming back, Rourke pulling the trigger once, then once more, then once again, the wildman's body rocking with each slug, spinning, stumbling, then falling over, forward, bouncing once, blood splashing from the arm and the chest as the body impacted.

Rourke, the Detonics still in his left fist, used the fist to push himself up, his right arm starting to get the feeling back. Another man was charging at him. He pumped the trigger—the Detonics bucked in his hand once, then once again.

Rourke wheeled, half stumbling, coughing still, his throat burning—half from the pressure of the strangler, half from the smell of Henderson's burning flesh.

A woman with a machete was rushing him. Rourke fired the last round in the pistol, her body taking the slug, reeling, falling.

The slide still locked back, Rourke jammed the pistol into his belt.

He flexed his right fist as he reached up awkwardly with his left hand to the Detonics under his left arm. His thumb coiled around the front strap of the grip, he ripped, the pistol coming free of the leather. He twisted the gun in his hand, worked the hammer back and started forward, toward Henderson.

The man Rourke had gutshot was getting to his feet, the torch still in his hand, the arm beyond the hand blackened where the flesh had singed in the heat of the pyre's flames.

The man swung the torch, Rourke stumbling back, firing the Detonics, hitting the wildman executioner in the face twice, the head exploding like an overripe melon hitting concrete.

On the ground near the base of the cross was a machete. Rourke wrapped his still numbed right fist around it, trying to find a way of reaching past the tongues of flame.

"Damn!" he rasped.

The flames were too high, too hot.

He pulled back, Henderson still screaming.

"Think! Think, Rourke—think, damnit," he shouted to the flames, to himself.

"Look out, John!"

Rourke wheeled, the Detonics in his left fist punching forward. It was Rubenstein, visible past the turned forward and down windshield of a jeep, the jeep bouncing and rolling from the far side of the ring of crosses.

Rourke shouted, "Paul—drive her into the base of the cross and jump clear—hurry!"

There was no answer, just something halfway between a wave and a salute, Rourke sidestepping, pulling the trigger on another of the wildmen, this one with a spear. The body lurched back and fell.

Rourke's right hand was working again—it pained but functioned. He dropped the machete, ramming the second Detonics into his belt beside the first one, swinging the CAR-15 forward, spraying out the magazine into the wildmen as they ran from the oncoming jeep.

The CAR-15 was empty and Rourke let it drop in its sling, drawing the Python from the flap holster at his hip, double actioning one of the 158-grain jacketed soft points point blank into the chest of one of the wildmen. He turned, the jeep snaking past him, one of the wildmen clambering onto the hood. Rourke pushed his right fist to full extension, double actioning another round from the six-inch, Metalifed Python, missing, then firing again.

The second shot caught the wildman on the hood of the jeep in the left side, the body rolling off, gone. Rourke jumped back, Paul's jeep crashing through the flames at the base of the cross, Paul jumping clear, rolling, coming up, his subgun firing into the wildmen.

Rourke snatched up the fallen machete from the ground, shifting the Python to his left fist, jumping the flames at the perimeter of the pyre, reaching the cross, Henderson screaming, his legs afire. Rourke dropped the revolver and the machete, lowering his hands into the damp ground and the light covering of snow, scooping up handfuls, putting them on the flames. There was a dead wildman near him.

Rourke snatched at the animal skin half covering the man, using it like a blanket, swatting at the flames, smothering them, then throwing his body over the animal skin to deny the flames the last of the oxygen they needed.

He pulled back the animal skin, the smell of burnt flesh nauseating him.

He found the machete, hacked with it at the ropes binding the ankles to the stem of the cross. Flesh fell away, stiffened, blackened.

But the legs were free, Henderson moaning incomprehensibly.

Rourke started for the ropes on the left wrist, recoiling for an instant—spikes had been driven through the palms of the hands.

He felt something, snatching up the Python from the snowy ground, firing it point blank into the face of an oncoming wildman.

The big Colt in his left fist, he hacked with the machete in his right—at the ropes tied around the wrists of Corporal Henderson.

There was a gutting hook near the base of the machete—or whatever its purpose, it looked like a gutting hook. Rourke started to work at the massive nail driven through Henderson's left palm—he stopped. He touched his hand to Henderson's neck, then set down the machete. He raised the left eyelid—Henderson had died.

Grasping the machete, raising to his full height, Rourke turned—a wildman raced toward him, a butcher-sized Bowie knife in his upraised right hand.

It was a sucker move, Rourke thought.

He stepped into the attacker's guard, batting away the knife with the six-inch barrel of the Python, then slashing the machete in a roundhouse swing, severing the attacker's jugular vein—the life had gone from the body before it plopped to the ground, spurting, splashing as the heart still pumped.

Rourke dropped the machete—Rubenstein's subgun was still firing.

Rourke could hear it.

He pumped the last two rounds in the Python into another of the wildmen, then holstered the revolver still empty.

A fresh stick for the CAR-15 from the musette bag—he inserted it up the well, stuffing the empty away.

He worked the bolt, pumping the trigger, taking out two more of the wildmen, using only six rounds.

He let the CAR-15 hang on its sling, taking one, then the other of the Detonics .45s—he rammed fresh magazines up the wells of both pistols, from the Six Pack on his belt, putting the empties in their places, filling the slots.

One pistol in each fist, he started forward—there were still men to save—men with mangled bodies, bleeding wounds—men who hadn't yet been set aflame.

He started firing, killing.

# Chapter 36

"No, damnit, Miss Tiemerovna—"

"Natalia," she nodded.

"All right—then no, damnit, Natalia," Gundersen shouted. "I'm not takin' a woman KGB major wearing a bathrobe and an arctic parka into a rubber boat for a shore party to investigate what sounds like a battle royal—got it?"

"Damn you," she shouted.

"Thank you very much for the good wishes—you can stay in the sail if you like—come on, O'Neal—let's launch," and Gundersen started across the missile deck and over the railing side cleats toward the rubber boat.

Natalia screamed after him. "Nyehvozmohznoh!"

Gundersen looked up as he took the ladder. "And what the hell does that mean, lady?"

"It is Russian—you are impossible!"

"Thanks again," and Gundersen's head disappeared from sight.

She shivered—she wore a hospital gown under the robe and the arctic parka only covered the upper half of her body, the wind blowing up under the robe.

Almost as if Gundersen could read her mind, she heard him shout, "And get that damn woman a blanket to wrap around herself before her legs freeze!"

"Aye, sir," a voice called back.

"Aye," she snarled.

# Chapter 37

He had fought his way to Rubenstein's side, the two men standing now, back to back.

"Gotta move on those crosses," Rourke shouted. "Get some more of them down."

"Of the six I freed," Rubenstein shouted over the steady roar of the high pitched subgun, "only two of them were able to move—one guy on the ground was using an assault rifle I liberated."

Rourke said nothing, eyeing the battleground—there were still dozens of the wildmen, attacking in small packs, sporadic gunfire coming toward them now. Then, "Let's get outa here—free the rest of the men to carry the ones who can't walk—fight our way back toward the beach."

Rourke started moving, Rubenstein backing as Rourke glanced toward him, covering his back, the barrel of the CAR-15 radiating heat as Rourke kept firing, the magazine well hot to the touch slightly as Rourke rammed a fresh stick up the well.

"I'm almost outa sticks, John," Rubenstein sang out.

Rourke shouted back, "Let's run for it—beat ya to the nearest cross," then started out at a dead run, keeping low, the CAR-15 spitting fire. The nearest cross had a man clinging to it who seemed half dead, blood dripping down his wrists and forearms but no spikes driven through the palms of his hands—massive lacerations instead.

"Lemme," Paul shouted, shifting the German MP-40 back on its sling, putting an open pocket knife between his teeth, then jumping for the cross's spar, reaching it, wrapping his blue jeaned legs around the stem and the man on it, then freeing one hand, sawing at the ropes. Rourke had retrieved his black chrome Sting IA and he hacked with it now at the ropes binding the ankles to the cross's stem.

"One hand to go," Rubenstein shouted.

"Dr. Rourke," the man called down from the cross. "God bless you both!"

Rourke stared at the face of the man strung to the cross—the irony of the words struck him, at once saddened him.

He held the man by the legs as Rubenstein tried guiding him down. The man's sweating, shivering body was covered with clotted blood from lash marks across his chest and back, stab wounds in his thighs and upper arms.

Rourke felt almost ashamed to ask. "Could you handle a gun—even from the ground?"

"Yeah—a gun—yeah," the man mumbled.

"Fine," Rourke nodded, rising to his full height, picking a target with an assault rifle. He started toward the wildman at a loping run, firing the CAR-15 as the man turned around.

Rourke was beside the body the next moment, wrestling the AR-15 from the dead man's grasp, searching the body—finding what he sought. Three spare twenty-round magazines.

He started back toward Rubenstein and the injured soldier—two of the wildmen blocked him, Rourke firing a short, two round burst from the CAR, downing the nearer man, the second man rushing him. Rourke sidestepped, snapping up the rifle butt, smacking against the side of the man's face. He wheeled half right, raking the flash deflector down like a bayonet across the exposed right side

133

of the neck. The man sank, Rourke dropping got his knees beside the first man, firing his CAR-15, assault rifle fire leveled at him now from the far side of the ring of crosses. Two of the wildmen—Rourke hitched the rifle he held to his shoulder, firing, one of the two men down, the second pulling back. Rourke grabbed up the M1 carbine the dead man near him had carried, searched the body under the rags and animal skins, found two thirty-round magazines in a jungle clip and was up and running again.

Still more than two yards away, Rourke hurtled the M-16 through the air, "Paul!"

Rubenstein caught it, wheeling, his High Power getting stuffed into his trouser band, the M-16 spitting fire into three men running toward the cross, handguns blazing.

"The Schmeisser was out, John," Rubenstein called.

Rourke nodded, saying nothing, dropping to his knees again beside the injured man.

"Here—use this," and Rourke gave him the M1 carbine and the spare, clipped together magazines.

He pushed himself to his feet, getting beside Rubenstein, stuffing the spare magazines, for the AR-15 into the side pockets of Paul's field jacket.

"We'll be back for you," Rourke shouted, starting toward the next cross, twenty-five yards away. As they reached it, Rourke dropped, Rubenstein beside him, heavy gunfire—assault rifles, shotguns, handguns, coming from the base of the next cross.

Rourke ducked behind the stem of the cross he was near, the rifle to his shoulder again, squinting under the scope across the sights, pumping the trigger once, then once again, then pulling back, one of the bodies dropping.

"Damn them," Rubenstein shouted. Rourke looked toward the next nearest cross. One of the wildmen was firing up at the crucifixion victim, the body twisting, lurching with the impact of each slug, then slumping— dead.

There was one more man—a cross fifty yards away on Rourke and Rubenstein's left—plus the man hung above them. Blood dripped onto the back of Rourke's hand—he looked up. The man who hung there was dead, a gaping hole in the right side of his head.

Rourke pushed himself up to full height, keeping as well behind the stem of the cross as possible, shouting to Paul, "Keep down!"

Rourke started to fire, emptying the stick toward the men at the base of the next cross, the CAR-15 coming up empty, Rourke ramming a fresh magazine home, firing it out, the men at the base of the cross starting to break up, running in different directions. Two of them ran toward the last cross—one man still lived hanging there.

Rourke started to run. "Come on, Paul." He reached to the shoulder rig, grabbing out one of the Detonics pistols with his left hand, the Detonics in his left, the CAR-15 in his right held just by the pistol grip. There was gunfire everywhere—as if somehow more of the wildmen were coming out of the woods. As Rourke raced toward the last cross, firing the CAR-15 into the wildmen's group, he could see that more were coming—perhaps late arrivals for the "fun" of the torture, perhaps from other camps nearby.

He stopped at the base of the cross, ramming another magazine into place for the Detonics he'd fired out, the CAR-15 empty, hanging on the sling at his side. He grabbed the second Detonics, one pistol in each hand, at hip level, firing toward the attackers.

Paul was already starting to climb the cross. Rourke heard him shout, "This one's dead."

Rourke glanced up once, then brought the pistol in his left hand to eye level, snapping off a shot at a wildman getting too close.

"Paul—get the men you released earlier—if any of them are left—meet me at the far side. I'll get the guy with

135

the carbine.''

''Right!''

Rourke glanced at Rubenstein once as the younger man jumped to the ground, then started to run.

Rourke ran as well. He was out of ammo for the CAR-15. There were only a few loaded magazines left for the Detonics pistols, the guns in each hand nearly empty.

He slowed his run, ducking down, catching up a riot shotgun on the ground.

His right fist wrapped around the pump, the Detonics from his right in his belt, he snapped his right hand down then up, the pump tromboning a round into the chamber, the spent plastic high brass shell popping out of the ejection port. Rourke tossed the shotgun up, catching it at the small of the stock, his fist wrapping around the pistol grip. He started to run again, firing out the Detonics in his left hand, then wheeling toward three of the attacking wildmen rushing toward him.

The riot shotgun—a Mossberg—in his right hand, he snapped the trigger, the gun bucking violently in his hand, the muzzle climbing. He slapped at the fore-end with his left hand, pumping it as one of the men went down. He fired the second round, jacking the slide again, chambering another round. He fired as the second man went down, nailing a third. He tromboned the Mossberg once more—the shotgun was empty.

A wildman was racing toward him with a spear made from a pole or piece of pipe and a long bladed knife.

Rourke flipped the shotgun in his hands, starting a baseball bat swing, hitting the spear carrier full in the face with the butt of the riot shotgun, then dropping it, running. Ten yards to go until he reached the injured man with the M1 carbine who fought from his knees at the base of the cross from which he had been hung.

Five yards to go, the man taking a hit, then another and another.

The Detonics in Rourke's right fist barked twice, one of the wildmen going down.

He fired again, hitting a second man in the chest, the body flopping back, spinning out and falling, the slide of the Detonics locked back, empty.

Rourke reached the man with the carbine, prying it from his hands, inverting the jungle clip. He pulled the trigger, three rounds firing when one should have.

The gun had been modified for selective fire.

Rourke pumped the trigger, one wildman down, then another and another.

He looked to the man on the ground beside him, trying to prop the man's head up against his thigh.

"Cole—Cole—"

"It's me—John Rourke," he rasped.

"Yeah—know that—Cole—ain't who he says he is—ain't Cole—you did me good, you and the other guy—did me—" The man coughed once, blood trickling from the corner of his mouth, the eyes open wide, staring, reflecting the light from the bonfire.

Rourke thumbed them closed, then got to his feet, running, firing out the thirty-round magazine in the carbine.

He was nearly at the far edge of the circle of crosses, could see Rubenstein with two other men, Rubenstein and one of the men half carrying the third between them.

The carbine came up empty as Rourke pulled the trigger for a short burst on one of the wildmen.

He had a rifle. It was a lever action. Rourke snatched it up, no time to search pockets for loose ammo. He cocked the hammer and pulled the trigger, nothing happening, then found a target. The last three fingers of his right hand in the lever, the first finger locked against the trigger guard, he started working the action, keeping his trigger finger stationary to automatically trip the trigger as the lever closed.

The rifle bucked in his hands, Rourke eyeing the brass as it ejected as he worked the lever forward—some type of pistol cartridge—likely .44 Magnum he guessed, not having time for a closer look.

He jerked back on the lever as a machete-wielding man raced toward him. The rifle bucked again, the body of the man with the machete folding forward at the waist, tumbling then still on the ground.

Rourke started to run again, levering the rifle at targets of opportunity, at last the tubular magazine coming up empty.

But he was beside Rubenstein.

"You got any ammo left for that AR?"

"Empty—"

"Makes an okay club," Rourke shouted, wheeling, lashing out with the lever action's barrel, catching a knife wielding wildman in the face. Rourke inverted the gun, to use it as a club, another man rushing them, but Rubenstein had the AR turned around and was halfway through his swing. The buttstock connected, the man's head snapping back.

Rourke started to run—"Let's get outa here—up into the rocks."

He slowed, two of the wildmen approaching, spears in their hands, both men crouched low.

Rourke swung the lever action, feigning, one of the spears snapping out toward him as he sidestepped, the rifle in his hands crashing around, impacting against the man's neck. Rourke backstepped, a shot nailing the second man. It was Rubenstein with the Browning.

"Still got a little left for this!"

"Save 'em till we need 'em!" Rourke started to move, stopped, the man on Rubenstein's far side taking a hit in the leg, going down.

"You get the other guy out," Rourke shouted, running back to the second trooper.

138

"I'll get this one."

Rourke dropped to his knees beside the man, the knee apparently hit, blood pumping from it between the man's interlaced fingers. Rourke shifted magazines in his pistols—counting the half spent magazines, he judged he had three dozen rounds left.

"Lean on me," Rourke rasped, hauling the man's left arm across his shoulders, holding the left wrist in his left hand to keep the man up, a Detonics pistol in his right hand.

The wildmen were consolidating—at least Rourke judged it as that looking behind him.

Had the men who tortured their victims on crosses had the slightest amount of organization, he realized full well he and Rubenstein would have been dead in the first minute of battle.

But they seemed intent on personal bloodletting rather than victory, using their knives rather than guns—they were insane, he thought absently as he hobbled under the added weight of the wounded man.

The man was talking. "My knee—my knee—Jesus help me—my knee!"

"Not much farther," Rourke lied, reaching the base of the rocks—but the rocks were still there to climb, Rubenstein now only a few yards ahead, helping his wounded man up into the rocks.

There would be little chance to run for it, but run for it they must, Rourke realized—to the beach, and hope that Lieutenant O'Neal would have dispatched another boarding party.

He heard a high pitched scream—a woman's voice. "Kill the heathens!"

Heathens—despite it all, a smile crossed his lips as he ran.

# Chapter 38

"Captain—the gunfire's pretty much died out."

"Hope those men haven't died out with it, O'Neal," Gundersen panted, pulling himself up over a breadloaf-shaped rock and starting for the next one.

Gundersen judged the distance remaining to the height of the rocks as some twenty yards—twenty yards that could well take another five minutes to traverse. "O'Neal—take your men and spread 'em out—both ends of the rocks. We get up there and there's an ambush waiting for us, don't want 'em having too easy a time of it."

"Like a pincer movement, sir—"

"Don't give me that Army crap," Gundersen laughed, panting, his breathing coming hard. He realized now—shifting his weight to pull up over another rock—what a soft life it was to be a submariner.

O'Neal was shouting orders, the men of the landing party fanning out. Gundersen silently wished he had Marines with him—he'd used Marines in a shore party once and despite the massive Navy-Marine Corps rivalry, he considered them consummate fighters.

He was nearly to the top of the rocks, to the ridgeline there and he stopped, leaning against a slab of flat rock, taking the Government Model .45 from the shoulder holster strapped across his chest, jacking back the slide. He still wished he hadn't lost the Detonics.

He raised the thumb safety, then turned toward the rocks again, inhaling deeply, resigning himself to the last part of the climb. As he started it, he shouted to O'Neal and the others, the words coming in gasps because of his breathlessness.

"We reach the—reach the top—con-consolidate on me and on O'Neal—consolidate on us before fanning out." He didn't know if that was proper tactics, but he didn't want his men too scattered. He reached up with his left hand, then his right, the pistol in his right hand scraping across the rock. "Kiss off the finish," he murmured, peering up over the ledge.

He could see Rourke, Rubenstein and two men—the men looked butchered and half dead—running, limping, pursued by what seemed like a hundred men who looked even more terrifyingly feral than the prisoners brought back to the submarine. They brandished knives, guns, torches. And faintly, as the running bands came even closer, he could hear shouts—savage cries. "Kill the heathens!"

"Holy cow," he swore. "Christ—"

# Chapter 39

Rourke dropped the man to the ground, turning toward the mob, a Detonics pistol, freshly loaded, in each hand.

"Paul—we can't haul these guys any further!"

"I know," Rubenstein's voice came back, sounding odd.

"If I don't get out—and you do—"

"I'll get back—I'll find them—I swear it to God, John—"

"And Natalia—"

"I'll take care of her—"

The younger man was beside him now—no rocks to hide in, nowhere to run, out in the open, the savage horde of wildmen running toward them brandishing spears, clubs, knives, a bizarre assortment of guns—and the torches lighting the night, their glowing brilliance leaving floaters on the eyes as Rourke watched.

"John—"

Rourke stabbed one of the pistols into his belt, his right hand going out, to Rubenstein's shoulder. He said nothing, just looked at the man—his friend.

He moved his hand away, retaking the Detonics .45 in his fist, his fingers balling on the checkered rubber of the Pachmayr grips.

Rourke had predetermined it—he would save one round, to shoot Paul if somehow it looked the wildmen would take him alive. It was better than the cross, far better.

He held the pistols at his hips, ready.

The mob was slowing its advance, the leaders or front runners—Rourke couldn't tell which—waving their torches in the air.

The mob stopped, then began to advance, slowly, at a determined walk. The isolated shouts and curses were gone, but the voices now becoming one voice, a chant, the words chilling his soul. "Kill the heathens! Kill the heathens! Kill the heathens! Kill—"

"John—remember how you used to tell me—trigger control?"

Rourke nodded, words hard to come for him, his throat tight. "Yeah. I remember."

"It's been like a second life anyway, hasn't it," the younger man's voice murmured, Rourke not looking at him.

"Yes."

Rourke turned to look at Rubenstein, the pistol—the battered Browning High Power—clutched in his right fist. His left hand, as if an automatic response, moved to the bridge of his nose, to push back the wire-framed glasses.

"It has—a second life," Rourke nodded, seeing his friend he judged perhaps for the last time.

The mob was less than fifty yards from them now, the smell of the torches acrid on the night air, the faces of the men and women who held them gleaming and reddened, glistening sweat.

The chanting of the mob had stopped.

One man stepped out of the front ranks, a torch in his right hand, a long bladed knife in the left, the torchlight glinting in streaks of orange and red from the steel—blood was there. He shouted, the crowd otherwise hushed.

"Kill the heathens!"

Rourke snapped the pistol in his right hand to shoulder height and fired once.

The 185-grain JHP brought the man down, the body

lurching into the crowd, the torch igniting the animal skin covering a woman near him. Her scream was loud, but died in the shouts of the mob as they broke and ran— toward Rourke and Rubenstein.

Rourke waited, remembering a line his father had quoted often, but only as a joke. It was no joke now. "Don't shoot until you see the whites of their eyes."

# Chapter 40

Rourke could see the whites of their eyes in the torchlit glare reflected from their steel. He opened fire, Rubenstein's pistol barking from beside him, the pistol sounding louder to him than his own guns, despite the difference in objective noise volume between .45 ACP and 9mm Parabellum merely because of the Browning's position relative to his ears.

The twin stainless Detonics pistols bucked, bucked again and again, bodies tumbling, spinning out, falling, more bodies swelling the ranks behind them—a wave, a human wave that seemed endless.

The Detonics pistol in his right hand was locked open, empty.

He fired the pistol in his left, the round slamming into the chest of a man less than twenty yards from him, the man going down, the slide of the second Detonics locking open, empty as well now.

Rubenstein's pistol was still discharging, Rourke changing to his last full magazines for both guns. He would have to scrounge the partially loaded spares.

As he raised the pistol in his right hand, Rubenstein's pistol suddenly still, the forward element of the wave, of the mob so near he could feel the heat of their torches, there was a shot burst, then another and another.

The wildmen—they were using their guns?

Another shot burst—M-16 fire as best he could tell,

bodies going down from the leading ranks of the wildmen storming toward them. Now shot burst after shot burst, automatic weapons fire ringing deafeningly across the rocky outcropping on which Rourke stood, Rubenstein beside him.

"John!"

Rourke glanced to his right, muzzle flashes coming from the rocks at the base of the ridge which rose then fell toward the beach. There were men, running from the rocks, M-16s in their hands, spitting tongues of fire in the night.

"Rourke! Doctor Rourke!" Rourke heard the shout but didn't look to find the source, instead turning his freshly loaded pistols at the mob, none of them advancing now, some screaming, fleeing, dropping their torches.

The pistol in his right fist—a shot into the head of a wildman still holding a torch, the head seeming to explode, the torch falling against it, the hair catching aflame. The pistol in his left—a woman, an assault rifle blazing in her hands toward the shore party—her chest seeming to sink into her as the body flipped back, spread eagling against a heavily bearded man who dropped his torch.

The pistol in his right—the man with the heavy beard who held the woman, his neck spouting a gusher of blood in the firelight.

The pistol in his left, the pistol in his right, his left, his right, his left, right, left, right, left—the slides of both Detonics pistols, the stainless steel gleaming dully in the torchlight of the burning faggots on the ground, bodies writhing there, were locked open, the guns empty.

"Rourke!"

He turned his head now—Commander Gundersen, running, a .45 in his right fist, two seamen flanking him, firing M-16s.

"John!" It was Rubenstein. "John!"

146

Rubenstein's High Power was licking flame into the night, the pistol at full extension in his locked fists, his body in a classic combat crouch, the 9mm double column magazine Browning barely rocking in his hands.

"Rourke!"

Gundersen was beside them, the two seaman dropping to their knees, firing their assault rifles as they spread prone on the ground, short, rapid bursts, spinning more of the wildmen from the mob, the mob breaking up, running.

"I've only got fifteen men—all I could spare from the ship—we gotta get the hell outa here."

"Wait a minute," Rourke rasped. He walked forward, staying clear of the field of fire from the two seamen, noticing others of the landing party drawing back now, consolidating on Gundersen.

Rourke found what he sought, wrestling an M-16 from the hands of a dead wildman, searching bodies on the ground for loaded magazines, finding a half dozen magazines, twenties and thirties and some of the non-Colt forties as he found a second M-16.

He started back toward Paul and Commander Gundersen, the two injured men now being helped away by the two seamen who had covered Gundersen's advance.

"We gotta get outa here, Rourke!"

"Right," Rourke nodded, handing Rubenstein an M-16, distributing the magazines evenly between them, but keeping the thirties for himself—he liked them better.

He dumped the partially spent magazine in his newly acquired assault rifle, ramming it into his open musette bag, the fresh magazines in his belt, his empty Detonics pistols already holstered. He worked the bolt of the M-16, kicking out the already chambered round, Rubenstein catching it, Rourke smiling as he did, then Rourke letting the bolt fly forward.

"Now we can travel," he whispered. Already, the mob of wildmen was reforming, coming—and it was still a long way to the beach.

# Chapter 41

Natalia shivered in the sail. She was cold, and the gunfire she now heard from the height of the rocks above the darkened beach chilled her more—was Rourke alive? Paul? There had been sporadic gunfire, then heavier gunfire—a firefight.

She felt—it was a man's word and she smiled at it—impotent. She could do nothing trapped on the sail in her damned robe, the blanket around her like an Indian squaw, her bones shivering, her teeth chattering.

She looked beside her—a young man, almost equally as cold, she guessed, his cheeks and the edges of his ears red tinged in the wind that blew across them both.

She looked at the M-16 the young man held, not to guard her but to guard the sail, to secure the submarine from possible boarders. There were nearly a dozen more men on the deck, bundled in peacoats, white sailors caps tucked down on their heads, M-16 rifles in their hands.

"Sailor—what did Commander Gundersen instruct you to do if the shore party couldn't get back?"

"He told the exec to pull out, ma'am—least that's what I hear, ma'am."

"What if the shore party is coming back, but under fire?"

"We're to guard the deck, ma'am—that's it."

"Not return fire to cover them."

"Against orders, ma'am," and he smiled.

She smiled at him, too, judging his height, his weight—if he fell, how could she best keep his head from cracking against the rail or on the steel plating of the sail's deck?

She edged slightly closer to him, her eyes watching the rocks, flashes of gunfire visible there in the darkness and flashes of—she couldn't tell what. There was a dull sounding roar, like the waves against the beach, but more indistinct—like a human chant.

Natalia shivered again, waiting.

# Chapter 42

Rourke walked backward, pumping short bursts from the M-16 toward the advancing horde of wildmen—they were firing back, perhaps galvanized by the loss of life their ranks had suffered, galvanized to fight as a unit and the gunfire was having some effect. One of Gundersen's landing party was down, dead, the body being carried slung in a fireman's carry by one of the other sailors, still another wounded in the left arm, but firing an M-16 with his right.

Gundersen was running, back toward Rourke as Rourke turned to see how close they were to the far side of the ridgeline. "I'm already getting my men down with those two crucified men—got three more helping them, then to get the inflatable ready and into the surf."

"They're gonna pick us off as we climb down the rocks on the far side," Rourke told Gundersen matter-of-factly. "Unless we break up—Paul can take three men and so can I—fire and maneuver elements to cover the rest of you getting down."

"Where the hell is Cole anyway?"

"Don't know," Rourke shrugged. He didn't care either. As long as the man wasn't guarding his back.

"All right—do like you suggested—pick your own men."

"Paul," Rourke shouted, the younger man firing a burst toward the wildmen, the wildmen moving in the low rocks on the top of the ridge, firing, advancing, firing.

"Paul!"

"Yeah!"

"Pick three men—fire and maneuver—take 'em as close to the edge there as you can, cover me until I get my men back twenty-five yards, then we'll lay down fire and you move back."

"Gotchya," Rubenstein called back.

As Rourke grabbed one of the sailors by the arm, then gestured to two more, Gundersen, already running ahead to get the rest of the men down, shouted, "Good luck!"

Rourke looked after him, but said nothing.

# Chapter 43

Rubenstein rammed a fresh stick into his liberated M-16, the rifle coming up to his shoulder, one of his three man squad to his left, the other two behind and slightly above him.

He looked to his right—the edge of the ridge was perhaps a foot and one-half away, perhaps less, the rocks below jagged, dark, unremitting, he thought.

To fall into them—

"All right," he shouted to his men. "When I open up, hold it to three round burst—maximum—pick specific targets or we'll run out of ammunition before we hit the beach and we'll need plenty to keep them off our backs while we load the boats. Everybody ready!"

It was a command, not a question—he smiled, amused at himself. He had never served in any army, but since the Night of The War considered himself objectively a veteran of much combat.

These three sailors—they looked to him, though all his own age, certainly little younger. They looked to him.

Leadership.

He settled the butt of the M-16 into the hollow in his right shoulder, his right elbow slightly elevated.

A man moved among the rocks, then another and another behind him. Gunfire was starting again. He squeezed the trigger of the M-16, letting it go forward almost instantly.

A perfect three round burst. He made another, then another, bodies falling behind his front sight. He found himself laughing as he fired—insanity? He had no time to consider that, he realized.

"Trigger control!" He shouted at the man next to him who'd let off seven shots in a burst. As he fired again, he laughed again, murmuring it to himself as well. "Trigger control—trigger control—trigger—"

# Chapter 44

Rourke pushed himself up, firing, Rubenstein's fire team under heavy assault rifle fire from the rocks above, on the last leg of the fight toward the beach—a fight it appeared they might lose, Rourke realized. There would be enough firepower to hold the wildmen back until they reached the surf, but unless a fireteam remained behind to cover the withdrawal, it would be hopeless—the boats would be shot out of the water.

Rourke pumped the M-16's trigger, even three-round bursts nailing anonymous figures in the darkness, snow still falling in heavy flakes, the skin of his bare hands on the M-16's pistol grip cold.

"Come on, Paul!"

Rubenstein's three men hit the beach, Rubenstein still in the rocks, firing.

Rourke ordered his own men. "Those three—join 'em and set up a firebase to cover loading the boats," and Rourke started to run, back into the rocks, Rubenstein pinned down now.

As he reached the edge of the rock field, he looked up—the wildmen were coming, seemingly uncaring of their own lives, coming. Rubenstein's rifle was blazing a hundred yards up in the rocks, glints of ricocheting bullets striking sparks in the night on the rocks around him.

Suddenly, Rubenstein's rifle stopped.

"Changing sticks," Rourke rasped, upping his pace, clambering over the rocks.

There was still no fire from Paul's position.

"Paul!"

Rourke screamed the name.

"Paul!"

"Go back, John—I'm outa ammo!"

Rourke quickened his pace still more, running across the flat rock surfaces, jumping from one to the next, then climbing again, narrowing the distance to fifty yards. He began firing, at targets of opportunity, shadows among the rocks, running as he fired, to draw the enemy fire and give Paul the chance to run for it.

"Paul!"

The younger man—Rourke could see him, up, running, one of the wildmen hurtling himself from the rocks. Rourke wingshot him with a three round burst, the body missing its landing, its purchase, falling, tumbling across the rocks, a scream echoing as the body soared past him.

Paul had his rifle inverted, the buttstock forward, swinging it, two more of the wildmen coming for him. Rourke watched as Rubenstein swatted one of the men away, then fired as the second man made to shoot, the body sprawling back.

"Paul!"

"Save yourself," Rubenstein shouted as he jumped, missed his footing and skidded.

Rourke couldn't see his friend for an instant, then the younger man was up again, running, the rifle gone somehow.

Rourke made to fire, one of the wildmen leapfrogging to the rocks less than three yards behind Paul, a machete in his upraised right hand.

The M-16 sputtered once and it was empty.

"Shit!" Rourke rasped—it had been his last loaded magazine.

He started up into the rocks, still brandishing the rifle, but the rifle all but useless.

Heavy fire—too heavy, was coming from the beach below, up into the night toward the ridgeline.

"Fools," he snapped—they would burn up the last of their ammo.

He glanced behind him once, into the surf—one of the boats was already away.

"Paul! Hurry it up!"

"I'm trying, damnit!" Rubenstein stopped on the flat slab of rock, Rourke watching as the younger man wheeled, his hands reaching out, shoving at the chest of the machete wielding wildman, throwing him back, off balance, the man falling.

Rourke had scrounged all the ammo from partially expended magazines—he had nine rounds left, all in the Detonics pistols, six in one, three in the other.

He reached for the lighest loaded gun now, dropping the M-16 into the rocks, hearing as it skidded away and fell. He thumbed back the hammer with his left hand, aiming the Detonics as one of the wildmen came up on Paul, Rubenstein less than ten yards away, the wildman holding an assault rifle. Rourke fired, the man going down.

"Get his gun! Get his gun, Paul!"

Rourke started edging back, covering the younger man as he disappeared among the rocks a moment, then returned with an M-16 and two magazines, jumping from the nearest rock, now less than three yards from Rourke.

The younger man started to shoulder the rifle, Rourke shouting, "Save it—we'll need it later!" Rourke started to run, retracing his steps along the rocks, slippery under foot as the snow continued to fall.

Two boats were away now—Rourke could see them battling the rolls and swells trying to get off the beach.

He stared out to sea—the dark silhouette of the submarine was visible, perhaps two hundred yards from shore—a good rifleman or a leader with good men under him could lay down a field of fire into the rocks covering the withdrawal from the beach—perhaps O'Neal would get to the decks in time, or Gundersen. At the distance, accuracy would be nil, but heavy concentrations of fire aimed high enough to provide against bullet drop—it might work. He jumped the last rock, half sprawling into the sand as a burst of assault rifle from above powdered the rock beside him.

Rubenstein was firing, a three round burst, then another, a scream coming from the darkness as Rourke pitched himself to his feet and started to run to join the fire teams.

He looked behind him once—the wildmen were filling the rocks—coming, inexorably coming.

# Chapter 45

It had been coming on toward sunrise for some time, the darkness turning to grayness, and in the grayness, she could see the wildmen—wildmen the prisoners had looked like, the returning men had described. She could see them swarming down through the rocks perhaps two hundred yards away.

"Sailor—I'm sorry," she smiled, her right hand snapping out in a knife edge, the heel hammering against the man's throat with calculated force—disorient him, perhaps knock him out—not to kill. His body stumbled, slipped, her left hand catching at the M-16, her right hand snaking toward his neck, easing his fall, her abdomen aching badly where the incision was as she stooped to ease him down.

She stood, her breath coming in short gasps with the pain. She shrugged, the blanket falling from her head and shoulders completely now, only the arctic parka and the robe to keep her against the cold.

She winked a snowflake from her left eyelash, then eared back the bolt on the M-16, letting it fly forward. The nearest of the rubber boats was still more than fifty yards from the submarine.

She stepped to the rail, pointing the M-16 skyward, firing a short three-round burst, her selector set to full auto.

Faces—the sailors on the deck, turned toward her.

"Those men in the boats—the ones still on the beach—they'll never make it if we don't do something. We can fire into the rocks, fire high so we won't hit our own men—lay down heavy fire. Three round bursts—keep it pouring in there—please!"

The faces were blank, or at best puzzled.

"Like this," and she snapped the rifle to her shoulder, firing over the railing toward the rocks beyond the beach.

She returned the muzzle to the rail, resting it there. "Like this—we can do it."

"Orders, ma'am," one voice called up to her. "We ain't sposed t'fire."

"Sailor," she almost whispered. "I'll kill the first man who doesn't—those are your comrades out there—only you can save them."

Natalia Anastasia Tiemerovna shouldered the M-16 again, her abdomen hurting badly from the unaccustomed exertion.

She pointed the flash deflectored muzzle at the sailor who had spoken.

He looked at her for an instant longer. "Where's Harriman, ma'am?"

"I knocked him out so I could steal his gun."

"Yes, ma'am," and then the sailor—she couldn't tell the rank, turned to the men who stared at her from a missile deck. "You heard the lady—if we're gonna disobey orders, may's well do a fucking good job of it!" And he looked up at Natalia.

"Scuse the language, ma'am."

"Think nothing of it, sailor," she smiled.

"Yes, ma'am," and he shouted again then. "Four of us up in the bow—two more up there with the lady, the rest on the starboard side—shoot high!" The sailor started to sprint across the missile deck, then suddenly all the men were moving.

Natalia, her abdomen still paining her, but warmth filling her suddenly, threw the rifle to her shoulder.

She could see no targets, but she could see the last defenders on the beach from their muzzle flashes. She aimed high, firing into the gray swirling snow.

160

# Chapter 46

Rourke looked over his shoulder, out toward the submarine's silhouette in the grayness and the swirling snow. There had been rifle fire—starting moments earlier. And now there was the fire of a deck gun, heavy sounding in caliber, silhouetted figures in the rocks above falling.

He glanced to Rubenstein, then to the six men around him.

"Let's catch those last two boats—come on!" He pushed himself up, starting to run across the sand, some of the wildmen now down from the rocks, pursuing him as he looked back, Rubenstein firing out the liberated M-16, nailing two of the men, then ramming the muzzle of the empty weapon into a third man's chest, leaving the man and the empty rifle lying in the sand.

Rourke splashed into the surf, the one man who'd remained with the boats hunkered down, his M-16 ready, the salt spray and foam washing over him. "Doctor Rourke!"

"Get in," Rourke snarled, taking the sailor's M-16, shouldering it and firing into the pursuing wildmen, covering for Rubenstein and the others.

"I only got the one clip, doctor!"

"Shit," Rourke snarled, firing another three round burst. He judged he had fifteen rounds remaining.

Rubenstein and the six sailors were coming, running into the surf, Rourke's legs freezing as the water soaked through his jeans, his boots. He fired again, switched to semi-automatic on the selector, pumping a single round into a wildman firing a riot shotgun. The man's body flopped backward into the surf.

Rubenstein ran for the body, snatching up the riot shotgun, firing point blank into the chest of another of the wildmen, then running for the rubber boats.

Rourke rolled himself over the fabric side and over the gunwales, prone now in the prow, firing the M-16 single shot. "Cast her off somebody," Rourke shouted, one of the six sailors hacking the rope with a jackknife, the rubber boat rolling up on a breaker, Rourke steadying his aim, nailing another of the wildmen.

Rubenstein's boat was casting off as well, the ends of the ropes that had secured the rubber boats to the shoreline floating on the foam near the rocks to which they were secured.

There was a boom, Rubenstein firing the riot shotgun, wildmen pursuing into the surf, Rourke firing the M-16, heavy gunfire from the submarine and the roaring of the surf all but deafening Rourke as he pushed himself up to his knees, spray lashing at his face, the icy cold of it making him shiver. He fought to control his hands, firing again, killing another of the wildmen.

He heard the shout—"John!"

Rubenstein's boat—the waves flooded over it, Rubenstein and the others rolling out, the boat upended. Rourke pumped the M-16, killing the man near the upended boat, the man giant-sized, his right hand hacking down with a machete as he stood in the surf, the compressed air of the rubber boat exploding out of the water, Rourke pumping the trigger of the M-16, once, then once again, then once more, the wildman's body slapping forward across the torn hulk of the rubber boat.

Rubenstein—Rourke could barely see his head bobbing in the waves, then suddenly Rubenstein was up, standing, the water chest high, a wave slapping him down—gone again.

Rourke stripped his bomber jacket away and the shoulder rig for the twin Detonics pistols, his left hand freeing the belt holster with the Python as he dove into the water, his body going flat to avoid hitting bottom, the breakers fighting him as he started toward his friend.

He pushed up, the salt spray pelting his face, his body racked with shivers from the chill of the water. More of the wildmen, on the beach, running into the surf. Rourke grabbed for the A.G. Russell knife inside his waistband, the little Sting IA black chrome coming into his palm as the nearest of the wildmen—spear in hand—lunged, Rourke's right fist feigned as he got to his feet in the water, his left snaking out in a straight arm thrust, the spear pointed knife, its steel shimmering in the water, biting deep into the wildman's throat.

The water ran blood red as the body flopped down. Rourke searched the surface—no Rubenstein. He ducked down, diving below the surface, his free right hand reaching to the bottom. Though it was nearly sunrise, the gray lightening above the surface, below the surface of the water, the swirling waves above him, tearing at him, it was dark.

A shape—darker than the rest. He started toward it, a machete breaking the water, the blade arcing past his face, inches away. He pushed himself up, two of the wildmen, one stabbing into the water with a spear, the second with the machete. Rourke lunged for the man with the machete, the long bladed knife slicing air past his throat, Rourke pulling back.

Gunfire, the man with the machete going down. Rourke looked to his right, toward the beach.

"Cole!"

He shouted the word, half a blessing, half a curse. Cole was running across the beach, his assault rifle spitting tongues of orange flame into the wildmen there.

The second wildman in the water—the one with the spear—turned toward Rourke, feining with the spear, then suddenly toppling back.

Rubenstein—the younger man, the right side of his temple dripping blood, stumbled forward into the water.

163

Rourke reached for him, the spearman thrusting again, Rourke wrenching the battered High Power from the holster across Rubenstein's chest, the gun empty he knew. The wildman took a step back, made to throw the spear. Rourke underhanded the knife from his left hand, the knife traveling the six feet separating them, imbedding to the base of the blade into the wildman's chest. Rourke dove toward the man, the High Power inverted in his right hand, the butt hammering down across the bridge of the wildman's nose, the skull there seeming to split.

Rourke fell back into the water, the knife's handle in his left hand as he wrenched the blade free.

He stood, a breaker crashing against him, knocking him back. He saw Rubenstein just as he went under, twisting his body against the force of the water, half throwing himself toward his friend. The bloodied pistol in his belt, his right hand free he reached—a short collar—the harness of the shoulder rig—he had Rubenstein.

Rourke pushed his feet under him, dragging the younger man up.

"Paul! Paul!"

"I'm—all—aww, shit—all right," he coughed, doubling over with the spasm.

Blood pumped from the head wound at his right temple.

Gunfire near him. Rourke wheeled, still supporting Rubenstein but nearly losing his balance, the knife in his left fist going forward.

It was Cole. "Come on, Rourke—give ya a hand with Rubenstein there!"

Rourke looked at Cole, his left fist bunching on the knife—"All right," Rourke snapped. "Where the hell were you when—"

"Trapped in the rocks—tell ya later!" And Cole grabbed at Rubenstein, slinging Rubenstein's left arm across his shoulders, starting toward the remaining rubber boat, the boat already visibly overloaded with the survivors of the destroyed craft as Rourke started after them.

# Chapter 47

Bullets—strays, the distance too great for aimed fire from the lower elevation of the beach—pinged against the hull of the submarine, Rourke taking Gundersen's right hand in his, letting Gundersen help him up from the rubber boat.

He had been the last man, his arms sore, numbed with cold from the paddling of the rubber boat, helping to fight against the breakers and reach the submarine, the boat so low in the water that the packed survivors had scooped water with their hands as each wave broke, swamping them.

"Doctor Rourke—I see why the president wanted you for this thing with the warheads—you should have been a field commander."

"War is stupid—fighting's necessary," Rourke answered, his voice a monotone—he was exhausted and knew it.

He shivered, crouching on the missile deck from the sporadic fire as the rubber boat was hauled up.

Gunderson, in cover behind the base of the sail, shouted, "Who the hell gave the order to open fire on the beach there—should court martial him—or give him a medal!"

The voice was quiet and Rourke looked up to the top of the sail. She held an M-16 in her hands, a half unconscious looking sailor standing beside her, leaning on the rail.

"I did, commander."

Rourke watched Gundersen's eyes. "If your doctor says it's okay, I'll buy you a drink, Major Tiemerovna—soon as we get this boat under the surface." Then Gundersen shouted. "Secure the deck gun— prepare to dive!"

Rourke stood up, getting to the cover of the sail, surprised that he could still move.

# Chapter 48

The "drink" had devolved to a glass of orange juice; Natalia sitting in her borrowed bathrobe beside Rourke in the officers' mess, Rourke feeling the pressure of her left hand on his right thigh through the blanket he had wrapped around him over his wet clothes. He sipped at his coffee—it was hot, almost scaldingly so—good to feel in his throat and stomach.

Gundersen walked in, sitting down, removing his cap and setting it on the table. "Doctor Milton says Paul Rubenstein is going to be fine—Rubenstein remembers trying to grapple with that wildman who overturned the boat—the butt of the man's machete took care of him. Milton doesn't think there's anything serious but he's keeping Rubenstein confined to bed for the next twenty-four hours just in case of mild concussion. Said you could check, but there really wasn't the need."

"He need any help with—"

"The wounded—Pharmacists Mate Kelly is patching up the lesser wounds, and Milton seems to feel he has the more serious cases under control. Those two survivors of the crucifixions—lots of cuts, bruises, lacerations—the only serious wound was Cole's man who got it in the knee—that knee's gonna keep him out of action for a long time, but should heal satisfactorily—at least that's Milton's preliminary diagnosis."

"Good," Rourke nodded.

Rourke looked across the table, at the far end to his left—Cole sat there, smoking, nursing a cup of coffee.

Rourke said nothing to him.

"Gentlemen—and major," Gundersen began. "We're going to have to find another area to try another penetration. The boat's ammo stores are seriously depleted, and more importantly the manpower. We lost six dead, have fourteen wounded in all."

"What about the wildmen we took prisoner?"

"Disassembled their cot springs, used them to slash their wrists—Milton nearly saved one of them, but the blood loss was too great." Gundersen sighed hard. "Suicide—what kind of people are these with such total disregard for their own lives—those attacks—they were suicide charges—I heard about them from the men in Korea years ago."

Rourke lit one of his dark tobacco cigars, his lighter too wet still to use, using a match instead. "Did Milton check the bodies for abnormal radiation levels?"

Gundersen nodded, then, "He thought of that too—maybe a death wish because they figured they were dying anyway. He autopsied one of the men while the battle was going on out there—aside from bizarre diet—nuts, berries, things like that, the man was perfectly normal. Physically," Gundersen added.

Cole, his voice odd, detached sounding, interjected, "We've still gotta get to those warheads—the hell with those wildmen or whatever they are—"

"Barbarism," Rourke interrupted. "Civilized men sunk to barbarism—so short a time. Some religion—has to be. They kept shouting, 'Kill the heathens.' Kept shouting it over and over. Half civilized, half savage—that business with the crosses, then burning people. My guess there's some leader who organized these people—survivors of the Night of The War, maybe a religious cult before then."

"There were many crazy religious cults in California—warrior religions and things like that," Natalia murmured. "Before the Night of The War—in KGB, there were plans to infiltrate some of the cults, perhaps use them to start civil unrest—Vladmir—"

"Vladmir?" Gundersen asked.

"My husband—he is dead. He—he, ahh—he believed that if the people of the United States could be made to fear their own homes, the safety of their own beds, they would be that much easier to conquer. Some agents were sent out—perhaps—" She let the statement hang.

Rourke looked at her, saying nothing, then knitting his fingers on the table, the cigar clamped in the left corner of his mouth. "It appears we have to go around or through these wildmen. Have to send a small, well-armed force to penetrate to that airbase. If there is any surviving complement there, we can use their help. Like as not they're under siege by these wildmen, too. If there was a neutron strike, there could have been some personnel in hardened sites or using hardened equipment who survived. Hopefully for our sake, Armand Teal was one of them. He was a good man. For an Air Force officer, a good ground tactician as well. We could use his help if we ever hope to get those warheads out." Rourke looked at Gundersen, saying, "I've got equipment to clean—the salt water. After that, I gotta sleep. I'm no good to anyone the way I feel now. If you can find another inlet further up the coast, then just surface to let us out, then dive again, maybe go to another inlet, attract a lot of attention, maybe we can slip through, past the bulk of the wildmen."

"Wildmen—Jesus," Gundersen nodded. "It's hard to imagine—"

"People are afraid," Natalia told him. "Afraid, and fear does a great deal. During the Second World War, people were easily reduced to depravities—informing on their friends and families, consuming human excrement to survive—"

Rourke interrupted her. "What she's saying is perfectly valid. Take the basic kernel of a fanatically violent religious cult—the cult offers a family, an ordered society, some element of protection. After the war—if you didn't join the cult, you'd be an enemy of the cult—a heathen, like they

169

shouted at us. Either join or die. And apparently to lose in battle and still live is the ultimate sin, or close to it.''

"But such savagery," Gundersen said, his voice incredulous.

"The vikings—at least some of them—I read once they'd set their beards on fire as they ran into battle to show their ferocity, their obsession with taking enemy life was greater than preserving their own. These people are like that. Wildmen is more than apt—savage.''

Gundersen held his face in his hands for a moment, then looked up, at Rourke, then at Natalia. "Have all of us done this—with our technology? Have we—ohh," and he sighed.

"I think it was Einstein," Natalia began.

"It was," Rourke nodded slowly, his voice little more than a whisper.

"He said that he didn't know what the weapons of World War Three would be when he was asked once. But he said the weapons of World War Four would be stones and clubs.''

Rourke looked at her, felt the momentary increase of pressure of her hand on his thigh. "Maybe," he said, his eyes closing, his head resting in his hands, his voice a whisper, "the dark times—or whatever they'll be called—maybe they've already begun."

# Chapter 49

Sarah Rourke opened her eyes—she looked at the wristwatch she had taken from one of the dead brigands after the attack on the Mulliner farm. It was a Tudor, the band hopelessly big for her, but the construction similar to a Rolex like her husband wore—made by the same company before the Night of The War as she recalled. It read a little after ten in the morning.

"Ohh—I was tired," she told herself, sitting up, banging her head on the tent pole above her.

She remembered—where she was—the refugee camp, the resistance commander David Balfry—how she had fallen asleep dreaming of her husband.

Pete Critchfield, the local commander who had, with Bill Mulliner, taken herself and the children to the camp had said there were showers.

She sat up on the blankets, searching through her kit—she found a clean T-shirt, a bra that didn't look too dirty and clean underpants. Mary Mulliner still slept—Sarah realized the trek would had to have been harder on the older woman. She decided to find the shower. She had no towel, but perhaps she could find one—or just be wet—to be clean was more important.

She gathered up the things as she stepped into her tennis shoes, stood up and stepped through the tent flap, finally rising to her full height. She noticed, suddenly, that without being aware of it, she had grabbed up the Trapper .45 Bill Mulliner had given her and replaced it in the belt holster on her hip.

"I'm going crazy," she told herself. She started across the camp, hearing children laughing, the sounds of play, from the far left end of the camp. She decided to find her children first—her own two and Millie Jenkins as well. She started through the camp.

More of the wounded, the habitually injured—they walked the impacted dirt of what had perhaps once been a front yard and was now a street. Their eyes—she could see no hope in them.

But the sound of the children laughing—it was nearer. At the furthest extent of the camp itself but still inside the security perimeter was a corral, white painted, though as she cut the distance, running her free right hand through her greasy-feeling hair, she could see the fence paint chipped and cracking.

She could already see Annie, and with her Millie Jenkins and more than two dozen other children, all seated on the ground, some older girls—teenagers, talking with them, the children laughing.

She stopped, not wanting to distract her daughter—the children were beginning to sing a song. Like many more things since the Night of The War, it held religious overtones—a hymn, but a cheerful sounding one, how Jesus loved little children.

She didn't see Michael, and as she started searching the crowd of singing children more closely, she noticed his total absence.

"I'm over here," she heard a voice say, the voice shockingly deep, but recognizable.

She turned, looking at her son—he was growing too fast, she thought absently, watching him sitting on the running board of a Volkswagen beetle, the car dirty, dented, but apparently still serviceable.

"What's the matter, Michael?"

He looked up at her, his brown eyes not smiling, the corners of his still childish mouth downturned, the leanness of his face more pronounced than she ever remembered having seen it. He had killed, he had saved her life and Annie's life—he had been a man.

"That's stupid—playing. Stupid."

"It's not stupid to play," she began, walking over to him. "Scoot over," and she nudged against him gently, sitting beside him on the running board of the VW.

"Yes, it is stupid—you know why?"

"No—tell me why," she told him.

"You know why."

"No—no, I don't. What is it? Just because you're a man when I need you, you figure you can't be a little boy anymore. Well—you are a little boy. You'll be a man soon enough—don't rush it anymore than you already have."

"That's not what I mean," he answered, looking up at her.

She folded her arms around him, drawing his head against her right breast. She heard the other children playing, the singing stopped, the children running off excess energy, chasing each other around the fenced-in corral.

She held her son very close—the little boy in him had died somewhere and she started to cry as she held him more tightly against her body.

# Chapter 50

Nehemiah Rozhdestvenskiy ordered the driver of the electric car to stop, then stepped out.

Its vastness amazed him.

The Womb.

Everywhere, men moved machinery and equipment, weapons, ammunition, food stores.

At the far end of the long, high-vaulted rock chamber he witnessed the coffin-shaped crates being transported one at a time because of their fragility on yellow, Hyster forklifts. There would be eventually two thousand of these, if time permitted. The first one hundred were already being unpacked, connected to monitoring equipment, being tested for functional reliability.

What they carried meant everything.

The rumble of electric generators being transferred on propane fueled trucks made an echoing sound.

"Comrade colonel—"

He looked at his driver.

"The future—it is here," he told the man. He told the polished stone of the walls—he told himself.

The Womb—he smiled as he thought of it. The most important strategic intelligence operation in the history of mankind—and at least for once, the code name was apt.

The Womb.

"Yes—drive on." He sat down, closing his eyes as the electric car took him ahead.

# Chapter 51

Rourke sat with the ship's armorer, the man reassembling an M-16 after having saturated it in a bath of Break Free CLP. Rourke had done the same with his own and Rubenstein's guns, getting to the salt water in time to prevent damage. He assembled Rubenstein's Browning High Power now, the finish a little the worse for wear but the gun wholly serviceable and no new evidence of rust or pitting. The armorer had aided Rourke in the detailed reassembly of the German MP-40 submachinegun—the older the weapon, somehow, Rourke had always noted, the greater the complexity of parts.

The six-inch tubed Metalifed and Mag-Na-Ported Colt Python .357 lay on the table before him, as did both Detonics stainless .45s, the CAR-15 and Rubenstein's MP-40 Schmeisser there as well—oiled, loaded except for the chamber (the revolver's cylinder was empty) and ready. A mink oil compound had been used on his boots and other leather gear, again preventing moisture damage.

The last item—the Russell Sting IA. Carefully, to avoid destroying the black chrome coating of the steel, he touched up the edge on the fine side of a whetstone, using the Break-Free as the lubricating agent here as well—he always preferred oil to water when the former was available.

He leaned back, breathing a long sigh, watching with one level of his consciousness as the armorer reassembled the trigger group of an M-16, and with the other level of his consciousness trying to think. The man Cole—there was something more to him than the swaggering, perhaps

175

cowardly, certainly self-serving too-rapidly-promoted military officer he purported to be. He tried remembering the words of the dying man—that Cole was not who he seemed to be.

It was a cliche, he realized, but dying men rarely did lie. Other than a last laugh on the world, what was there to gain from it?

The original orders Rourke had seen. They had clearly indicated to him that Cole did indeed carry presidential orders—but orders for whom?

More and more, things seemed to point to Cole being someone other than Cole.

Rourke leaned forward in the chair, beginning to load 230-grain Military Ball .45 ACP into the Detonics magazines. At the Retreat, he had large amounts of 185-grain Jacketed Hollow Points stored.

"At the Retreat," he murmured to himself.

Where he wanted to bring Sarah, Michael, Annie—Natalia, too? And Paul Rubenstein.

He smiled as he whacked the spine of a fresh loaded magazine against the palm of his hand to seat the rounds, then began to load another magazine.

He had been a man who had habitually done things alone. He had a wife, two children. He now had a woman who loved him, whom he loved. And he had a friend so close as to be a brother.

Rubenstein—the wound in his head had not proven serious, nor had any signs of concussion been evinced during Doctor Milton's twenty-four hours of observation.

In a few hours, the submarine would surface, he and Paul and the enigmatic Cole and others would start cross country to Filmore Air Force Base, to find the warheads.

That there would be further fighting with the wildmen—whoever they were—was obvious to him. Natalia had been grievously wounded, near death. Paul had been wounded in the last battle.

He had escaped it all—so far. There was no time for him

176

to be injured. The skies became progressively redder, the weather progressively more bizarre. The thunder which rumbled in the skies was so much a part of day-to-day existence that he barely noticed it, primarily noting it at all by its occasional absence.

He tried to remember—had it thundered during the time on land. But then it only seemed to thunder during the daylight hours. There were books at the Retreat—if he could find Sarah and the children, perhaps there could be time to study his books, to learn what was happening, to prepare somehow.

Time—he glanced at the Rolex. Time had become a way of keeping score only.

# Chapter 52

Two reports troubled him. He stuffed his feet awkwardly into his shoes, standing as he pushed away from his desk. Both reports were related, really.

General Ishmael Varakov—he read the sign on the front of his desk in his office without walls in what had been the Natural History Museum in Chicago. "Supreme Commander, Soviet North American Army of Occupation."

"Supreme commander," he muttered. If he were as "supreme" as the sign indicated, the two reports would not have concerned him as greatly.

He started to walk across the great hall and toward the nearer of the two staircases which led to the small mezzanine, so he could better overlook the main hall.

The first report concerned additional data on the American Eden Project and the related post-holocaust scenario which had necessitated the creation of the Eden Project from the very beginning. Had he been a man given to profanity, he realized he would have used it. Where was Natalia? He had sent her with the Jew, Paul Rubenstein, to get the American Rourke, to give him the note.

He started up the stairs toward the mezzanine, his feet hurting. He scratched his belly once under his unbuttoned uniform tunic. Natalia and the young Jew had been dropped by plane near "The Retreat," the place the American Rourke had.

Perhaps Rourke would not come. The obsession—a laudable one as obsessions went—with finding his wife and children. But, surely he thought, a man such as Rourke could not ignore the letter.

Perhaps—it was a possibility—the ghost-like Rourke, the man neither brigand killers nor Soviet Armies had been able to capture or murder, was somehow dead.

What would Natalia do?

She would return—as Rourke would have done—to learn the rest of the information, what she could do. The young American Jew—he would come with her.

As Varakov stopped at the mezzanine railing, slightly out of breath, weary, he wondered if perhaps all of them had been killed. Rourke, Rubenstein, his niece Natalia.

"What will I do then?" he murmured.

"Comrade general?"

The voice was soft, uncertain. He turned. "Yes, Catherine."

"Comrade general," the girl began. "These papers—they require your signature."

"Hmmph," he said, turning away, studying the figures of the mastodons which dominated the center of the great hall. "Soon, Catherine—we shall be like them."

"Comrade general," she began again, a long silence ending. "Comrade general—what is it—might I ask, Comrade general—what is it which seems to—to trouble you?"

He did not look at her—she was pretty, however plain she made herself appear intentionally.

"Catherine. More scientific data which greatly disturbs me, which shall profoundly influence us all. That is one report. And a second report. The KGB, which is stockpiling raw materials, equipment—everything you might imagine and many things, child, which you could not—one of their convoys was attacked by the American resistance near some city called Nashville. There is a resistance stronghold which Rozhdestvenskiy has committed Army forces to destroying —against my policies because there are women and children there. And without even asking my permission. He does not need it anymore, child."

179

He looked away from the mastodons, studying her face—the gentleness of her eyes.

"Catherine—I have never before stared death so closely in the face. Go and prepare for me coffee, child."

He started away from the railing, listening to the clicking of her heels, noting her skirt was still too long. He tried not to look at the mastodons—there would be little but bones to look at soon enough.

# Chapter 53

Jacob Steel, she thought, was perhaps a talented minister. He was not so talented as a doctor.

"Here—I'll tie that," she told him.

Steel looked up from the dressing he had attempted twice to secure, his gray hair falling across his forehead, his glasses smudged on the lenses. He smiled. "You've realized I'm a klutz, Mrs. Rourke. The only reason I learned anything about medicine in the first place was because when I was drafted, I was a conscientious objector. Had to find something to do with me—I couldn't type. I was starting to worry about you. Most people who've worked as my nurse have discovered my ineptitudes far sooner."

She felt herself smile as she secured the dressing. "I was just too polite, I guess, Reverend."

"Hmm—but I see you can do that quite well. Your husband's a doctor, is he?"

She looked up, but Steel hadn't waited for an answer. He had already moved to the next patient. She arranged the covers of the man on the ground by her feet, then stood, following Steel.

"Yes," she answered belatedly.

"Yes, what?"

"He's a doctor," she said.

Steel looked away, then back to the patient. The woman's burns were not healing. "Are those sheets sterile?"

Steel looked up at her.

She smiled. "That was a silly question, wasn't it?"

"Yes, Mrs. Rourke—it was a silly question. Nothing here is sterile. Except me—I caught the mumps from my daughter five years ago," and he laughed.

"How old is she—" She caught herself.

"Now? She's dead. My wife's dead. My two sons are dead. Our house is gone—wasn't really our house. Belonged to the church. Church is gone, too. I was away. Chattanooga was neutron bombed."

"I know," she answered quietly.

"Realize how many fires start in a given day—just your regular ordinary fires? I don't know how many myself, but I bet plenty. Fire started in the garage of the house across the street from the church—don't know why, but it looked like it started there. Spread across the street somehow—must've been the wind. Burned the church, the house. My wife and the children—woulda been dead by then anyway."

"I'm—"

"You're sorry," he interrupted. "I know you are. Pretty soon we're gonna run out of enough sorry to go around."

Reverend Steel pulled the blanket up over the woman's face. "So much for sterile sheets, huh?"

Sarah Rourke pulled the blanket down, closing the eyelids with her thumbs.

# Chapter 54

Rourke heard the knock, looked up as he called, "Come in."

The door opened.

"Mind if we talk, Doctor Rourke?" Gunderson asked.

"Not a bit," Rourke told him. "You don't mind if I finished getting dressed?"

Rourke stood up, walking stocking footed across the cabin, getting his combat boots and sitting down again, stuffing first his right foot, then his left foot into the leather. He began to lace the right one. "What do you want to talk about?"

"Couple things. Major Tiemerovna for openers. She wants to go along."

"She's too weak," Rourke told him, looking up. "Too dangerous anyway."

"I'm letting her go—"

"Bullshit," Rourke told him.

"See, it doesn't matter to me that she's a Russian—she's not going to do anything to jeopardize you. So I can worry about her sense of duty to mother Russia after you find the warheads. She wouldn't take you on—she'd wait and take me on for them. You're going to need all the backup you can get."

"Your Lieutenant O'Neal—pretty good man. I'll have Paul—Paul Rubenstein."

"Yeah," Gundersen smiled. Rourke began tying his left boot. "But you'll also have Cole and three of his men. He wants to kill you as soon as you get to the missiles, maybe before then. Everybody talks about you as a smart man—seems like it'd be kinda dumb for you to have missed that.''

"I haven't missed it," Rourke smiled, looking up, then looking back to his boots. He stuffed the ends of the bootlaces into the tops of his boots, then stood up.

Rourke walked back to the bunk, taking a clean blue chambray shirt from where he'd set it earlier, pulling it on. "Rubenstein and Major Tiemerovna—been talking with both of them a lot. Seems like there's nobody better with a gun or knife or in any kinda fight than you—"

"They exaggerate a lot," Rourke told him.

"Understand the three of you fought a lot as a team."

"We've done a few things," Rourke nodded.

"She's going. So, you walk a little slower, put on a few less miles per day. The warheads have waited this long, they can wait a little longer. She's got every reason in the world to kill Cole—can't say I blame her. What started it between them?''

"He told her he was going to put her under arrest. She told him to go to hell. He went to slap her—she flipped him. She could take on half your crew at once. She's one of the best martial arts people I've ever seen. Most women who are good in martial arts couldn't compete with a man nearly as good—the strength factor. She's the exception. She can move faster, think faster—"

"And then one of Cole's men shot her?"

"Yeah," Rourke said through his teeth.

"I gave her her guns back—you don't want her to go, you try takin' 'em away from her. Funny thing," and Gundersen looked down at the floor a moment, then Rourke watched his eyes as he looked up. "That Captain Cole—got orders signed by President Chambers, and she's admittedly a KGB agent. We're at war with Russia. Thing that's funny—asked myself why I trust her more than him.''

"One of his men," Rourke began, his voice low. He

stood up, stuffing his shirt into his pants, then closing his pants and his belt. "Before he died." Rourke picked up the double Alessi rig, the holsters empty. He raised his arms, letting the shoulder holsters fall into place. He picked up one of the Detonics pistols, working the slide, chambering the top round off the magazine. Slowly, carefully, he lowered the hammer, beginning to insert the gun in the holster under his left armpit. "One of his men told me before he died—Cole isn't who he says he is, whatever the hell that means." Rourke repeated the ritual for the second pistol, holstering it as well. "Could be those aren't presidential orders—looks like Sam Chambers' signature though."

"Major Tiemerovna—she'd have told you if Cole were a Russian."

"If she knew—since she started helping me, she's been coming under suspicion from her own people—nothing so much she's talked about, just what she hasn't talked about."

"You saying Cole could be a Communist and she wouldn't know?"

"She's KGB—there's still the GRU, lots of initialed organizations in Soviet Intelligence. And maybe it's something else. Can't see why the Russians would recruit a U.S. nuclear submarine to do this—why not land some troops?"

"Maybe they want to fire the missiles—maybe at China—use this as a surprise base—so the Chinese won't pick them up on long range radar."

"Four hundred and eighty megatons is enough to destroy a lot—maybe a really large city totally destroyed. Not enough to stop the Chinese though. Understand they're giving the Russians a hard time of it. But a plan like that'd be stupid."

"I tried contacting U.S. II—electrical interference in the upper atmosphere must be too strong for my radio equipment. You say the word, I'll pull the plug on Captain Cole and throw him in irons."

Rourke laughed, securing the Sting IA in its sheath on the left side of his belt inside the band of his Levis. "You really still have irons on board ships?"

"Well," Gundersen laughed. "Figure of speech. You get my drift, Rourke?"

"Yeah," Rourke nodded. "No—" His teeth were clenched—he could feel them as he spoke. "No—Cole's a ringer, or a Communist—or maybe something else—I'm sure of that. But we'll never find out what's going on unless we let him play out his hand."

"You play poker much, Doctor Rourke?"

"Used to play a lot with my kids—they'd always win," Rourke answered.

"Well—heard this line in a western once—you're drawin' against an inside straight—with Cole, I mean. He knows what he's doing—enough to leave his own men strung out there while you and Rubenstein tried saving them, then show up just in time for the last rubber boat out. It's important that he gets to the warheads—"

"And I'm the one Armand Teal will believe. He can't touch me until we reach Filmore Air Force Base and find out if Teal's still alive. I'm safe 'til then. All I gotta do is worry about those crazy-assed wildmen."

Gundersen stood up. "That's why she's going with you—for after you reach Filmore."

"I don't want her along—those stitches—"

"You told me six hours ago her stitches were nearly healed. She was practically back to normal."

Rourke licked his lips, buckling on the flap holster with the Python. He said nothing. Gundersen left.

Rourke looked at himself in the mirror—three handguns, a knife. It wouldn't be enough.

# Chapter 55

John Rourke squinted across the water—the submarine was already pulling out to deeper water, then would dive to resurface near the original site of the battle with the wildmen. To draw them off, he and Gunderson hoped.

Rourke reached under his brown leather bomber jacket, took the dark lensed aviator style sunglasses and put them on.

He chewed down on the stump of cigar in his mouth.

It was Cole. "You ready, Doctor Rourke?"

Natalia—her eyes so incredibly blue, her skin more pale than it was always. She looked at him, and so did Rubenstein. Rourke looking past them at Cole, answered, "Yeah."

Rourke reached down to the gravel beside his feet, snatching up the Lowe Alpine Loco Pack. He shifted it onto his shoulders, reaching under his bomber jacket and rearranging the straps from the shoulder rig.

"I take it due north a ways," Cole called out.

Rourke looked at Cole, then started to walk, Natalia and Rubenstein flanking him.

Her pack was light, but he knew that soon he or Paul would wind up carrying it.

"Due north?" Cole called again.

Rourke kept walking, through his teeth, the word barely audible, "Yeah."

# Chapter 56

David Balfry looked up from his desk, as though startled. She thought that was silly. He'd sent word he wanted to see her, she'd knocked before entering the room in the farmhouse, he'd told her, "Come in, Sarah."

She stopped in front of his desk, suddenly feeling grubby. She pulled the blue and white bandanna from her hair, shook her head to relax her hair.

"Sit down, Sarah," he told her smiling. "Got some news about your husband."

She sank into the chair. "He's all right?"

"I don't know—no reason to assume he isn't," and Balfry smiled, gesturing behind him out the window. "No more or less all right than anybody else these days."

"What—what is—"

"Close to three weeks ago—your husband left U.S. II headquarters before it moved off the Texas Louisiana border. He was with a younger man—a man named Paul Rubenstein. Seems they've been hanging around together ever since the Night of The War. And he was with someone else."

"Who?"

Why did she ask that, she asked herself. "Who was he with?"

"A Russian woman—major in the KGB. Natalia—Natalia something," and Balfry looked through the papers on his littered desk. "Natalia Tiemerovna—middle name Anastasia. Her husband was the head of the KGB in America here—until your husband gunned him down on the street—while ago in Athens, Georgia. Intelligence sources indicate the woman showed up in Chicago—that's Soviet Headquarters for the North American Army of Occupation—"

"I know that," Sarah nodded.

"Showed up in Chicago—without your husband or this Rubenstein character. Then she disappeared. Maybe to rejoin your husband."

Sarah licked her lips. "Russian woman."

Balfry threw down the paper in his hand—contemptuously, she thought absently.

"Doctor Rourke might be dead—maybe—"

"What?" she asked, not looking at Balfry.

"Look, Sarah—you're a beautiful woman. Who the hell knows how much time any of us have left." She heard the sounds of his chair scraping across the wood of the floor. She heard his footsteps—he was coming around the desk.

"Sarah," his voice purred to her. She looked up; David Balfry crouched in front of her chair, by her knees, his hands holding her hands against her thighs. "Sarah—he probably figures you and your children are dead. He's done what any normal man would do—taken up with somebody else. This Russian woman. He's not coming because he's not looking."

Sarah looked into Balfry's eyes. "I—I have to get—to get out of here."

She stood up, stepping past him as he stood, turning away from him, starting toward the door. She felt his hands, the fingers strong, pressing into her upper arms. She felt him turn her around.

She looked at his chest, not his face.

"Sarah—" He drew her close to him. She could feel his breath—his clothes smelled like his pipe tobacco.

She felt his hands—they moved to her face, cradling her. She looked at his eyes.

His mouth.

It opened slightly as he bent his face toward her.

His lips—they were moist. There was strength in the way he crushed against her mouth.

Her arms—she moved them around his neck. She leaned her head against his chest.

"Sarah—you're a woman. You need a man to care for you—let me care for you," she heard him whisper. "You've been brave beyond what most men could do—let alone a—"

She pushed away from his chest, stepped back, her hands groping behind her, finding the doorknob. "A woman?" she rasped. "Just what the hell is so damn wrong with being a woman? I should fall over dead in a faint when somebody shoots at me? I should let my children die because I'm crying and can't do anything to help myself? A Russian woman—fine. But he's still looking for me. I'm still looking for him. If there's a Russian woman—Natalia whats-her-name—whatever the hell she is—then fine. He'll tell me about her. And if we never see each other again—what should I do? Give away everything in myself to you—or somebody else?"

She found the doorknob—finally. She twisted it open, breaking a nail on it.

"Damn," she muttered.

"What?" Balfry asked her.

"Go to hell," she told him. She ran through the doorway.

# Chapter 57

She was tired. "Paul—you asked to take my pack—take my pack—please," she said.

Rubenstein turned toward her. She stopped walking, feeling herself sway a little.

Rourke asked her. "You all right?"

"Of course she isn't all right—takin' a damn Commie woman with us was fuckin' stupid, Rourke!"

She watched Rourke—he closed his eyes. He opened them—he bit down hard on the stump of cigar in the left corner of his mouth—despite the cigars, his teeth were white, even.

"No, John—I can—"

"I know you can," he said through his teeth.

He turned around. She could see Cole's face past his back. Rourke was shifting out of his pack.

"You want me to take your pack, too," Rubenstein asked, trying to make a joke, she thought. It wasn't funny.

Rourke dropped the pack. "No," he said quietly.

"We havin' a damn rest break here—should I tell everybody the smokin' lamp is lit?"

She watched Rourke, the muscles in the sides of his neck.

"Cole—I make it we've got a day's march left to Filmore Air Force Base and Armand Teal—but I just can't take another day of your mouth."

She looked at Cole—he didn't move. Then, "Yeah—well, too fuckin' bad, Rourke."

Rourke shifted his shoulders. She could hear the zipper in the front of his bomber jacket opening. "I thought you'd say that,'' she heard Rourke's voice murmur.

"What?"

"Thought you'd say something like that," Rourke said again, louder this time.

"John," she whispered. "Leave it alone."

Like he'd told Rubenstein with the back pack—"No."

"You lookin' for a fight, Rourke?" Cole shouted, laughing.

Natalia watched Rourke's head—it nodded once, slightly. She heard him say, his voice barely audible, "Yeah."

"Well," Cole smiled. "Well—you gonna take off your coat and your guns?"

"Won't need my guns—and no sense taking off my jacket for something that won't take much time."

"Wise ass, huh?"

Rourke said nothing. He started walking, slowly.

"John!" It was Rubenstein.

"I know," Rourke answered slowly, still walking, toward Cole. "But it can be your turn next time."

He stopped in front of Cole. Natalia saw movement at the corner of her right eye—Rubenstein setting down her pack, halving the distance between them. She rested her right forearm across the M-16 she carried slung cross body, her forearm just ahead of the carrying handle.

"Now look, Rourke—we got a job to—"

"Shut up," she heard Rourke say.

"The hell—" She saw Cole move, his right fist drawing back. Rourke sidestepped, turning half away from Cole, Cole's left hammering forward, Rourke's left foot snapping out—a double kick into Cole's midsection and chest. Cole stumbled back, Rourke bringing his left foot down, wheeling, his right foot snapping out, catching Cole in the chest and the left side of the face.

Rourke didn't turn around—he started walking. Back toward her.

She smiled—Lieutenant O'Neal was trying to stifle a laugh. He wasn't doing a good job of it.

# Chapter 58

"What's the matter, Momma?"

She looked up, Michael slightly above eye level as she sat on the running board of the old Volkswagen beetle. The irony of where she sat, Michael coming to her to ascertain what was wrong, the complete role reversal—it was not lost on her.

"Nothing—not really."

"I saw you come out of the house—is it Professor Balfry?"

"Sort of," she told her son, not really knowing what else to tell him.

"Daddy'll find us—especially here. All the resistance fighters going in and out all the time—all of the stuff goin' on here. He'll find out that we're here and come and get us."

She looked at her son—his eyes. She wanted to ask—why are you so sure? But she looked more deeply into his eyes, watched his face—she didn't think his eyes were light sensitive like those of her husband. He didn't squint against the light like John had always done—like John did. But he looked enough like his father to be his clone.

"When do you think Daddy will find us?" she asked instead.

"Probably not for a while yet. He's gotta first find out where we are, then he has to get here to get us. Might be a while yet. Maybe a few weeks."

She hugged her son to her. "Maybe in a few weeks," she whispered, believing it then.

"Momma—is everything—"

"Fine," she whispered, not letting go of him . . .

Millie Jenkins had left the refugee camp with Bill Mulliner and his mother—to pick blackberries. Michael hadn't wanted to go. He didn't like blackberries and liked the thorns less. Annie had gone with them though.

Sarah sat by the edge of camp with Michael, the wounded and injured under Reverend Steel's care for the moment. "What are you thinking about?" she asked her son.

"I don't know," and he laughed. She hadn't seen him laugh for a while.

"I like seeing you laugh. Your father doesn't laugh much. You laugh more. That's good."

"What'll we do after he finds us?"

She folded her left arm around the boy. "I guess—well, I don't know."

"Go and live in the Survival Retreat?"

"I guess so—at least for a while. Until the Russians are forced to leave, maybe. Maybe after that we can find a place and settle down there—just like pioneers," she added, her voice brightening. "Build a cabin—get some horses again. Maybe grow our own food. Like that?"

"No electricity."

"Your Daddy is pretty smart—he can probably find some land near a fast running stream and make our own electricity. Eventually, the cities will start up again and the factories—make things we can use."

"Will Daddy go back to work—and be gone all the time again?"

"I think—I don't know. It'll be a long time before we get rid of the Russians—"

"I hate the Russians," the boy said with an air of finality.

"You shouldn't," she said after a moment. "They're people, just like we are. Very few of the Russians are really Communists—it's the Communist government. They run Russia—they started the war. You shouldn't hate the

Russians.''

"Well, I hate the Communists then.''

"Well—I don't think it's going to hurt the Communists half as much as it's going to hurt you if you do.''

She looked at him—he was looking at her. "What do you mean?''

"Well—we've gotta fight the Communists. We've gotta win. But if they make us all live for hate, then maybe they'll win—even if we kick them out of our country. If we love freedom—being free to do what we think is right—it has the same effect as hating the Communists—but a good thing, not a bad thing. Hate won't do us any good. First thing you know—we'll spend all our time hating and we won't have time to fight the Communists and win. Like that.''

"Maybe that's like telling a lie," he told her, his voice very serious sounding, his eyes hard. "You know—you spend so much time telling lies you can't remember what's the truth.''

"Maybe," she nodded. "Maybe.''

She reached into her pocket, found the liberated Tudor wristwatch and checked the time. "I've gotta go and help Reverend Steel—but I'll see you at dinner tonight—okay?''

The boy smiled. "Okay—I'll walk you over there!''

"Okay," she smiled.

"I'll help you up!'' The boy was standing already and reached out his hand, Sarah taking it, letting Michael help pull her to her feet.

"Ohh—you're getting stronger all the time—you know that?''

"You wanna feel my muscle?''

"Okay," she nodded, the boy raising his arms in the classic iron pumpers pose.

"Which one do you think is bigger—stronger? I think it's my right arm.''

She felt the right arm, then the left—carefully. The biceps were hard, however diminutive. She felt the right one again. "I think the right one is stronger, too—but that

195

makes sense. You're right handed."

"Yeah," he nodded.

"Can I hold your hand?"

"Okay," he smiled, letting her take his right hand in her left.

They started to walk.

The last afternoon sun was low, the sky already reddening—the redness which seemed imperceptibly to increase bothered her—perhaps John would know why. She looked at Michael—he was tall, strong—she loved him.

She felt the pain before she heard the shot. She looked down—her left hand and his right were covered with blood.

"Michael!"

She smudged her right hand across their hands—the fleshy part of her left hand had a deep cut—it burned. The upper portion of Michael's right wrist, near where it joined the hand—a gaping cut there as well.

"Michael!" She dropped to her knees, gunfire everywhere now around her, ricochets humming maddeningly off vehicles and tent pegs and cooking pots. There was a whooshing sound. And an explosion to her far left—near the tent where some of the sick were housed.

The tent burst into flames.

A whirring sound—cutting the air.

She looked skyward—a helicopter—another helicopter —like the kind she had seen before, red stars painted over U.S. symbols—the Russians.

Michael's wrist. "Can you move it—"

He was holding back tears. "Yeah—it hurts!"

"Does it hurt to move it?"

"No—it hurts—hurts here," and he touched at the cut, tears welling in his eyes.

She ripped the bandanna handkerchief from her hair, binding it around Michael's wrist. The fleshy edge of her own left hand. She wiped it against the left thigh of her jeans, cleaning away the blood for an instant—her fingers moved, her wrist moved.

196

"Ohh, my God, were we lucky!" She pushed herself to her feet, grabbing the little boy by the shoulder. "Run, Michael—hurry!"

The helicopters filled the air like hungry insects above her, machinegun fire ripping through the dirt camp streets, men, women, children—running—dying.

The tent where her gear was—she needed to reach it.

"Come on, Michael—hurry—run!" She could see the tent, gunfire hammering the ground around it. Beyond the tent, at the farmhouse, she could see David Balfry, an assault rifle in his hands, blazing skyward. She heard the rumble of the trucks—

She looked behind her. The furthest end of the street— Soviet troops, pouring from trucks, rifles in their hands, women, children—the resistance fighters—going down.

"Momma!"

"Gotta get to the tent!" She screamed the words, fear gripping her—she turned, seeing more of the Soviet troopers now, running down the street, killing, killing— killing everyone. Reverend Steel—he was outside his tent, holding a cross in his hands with a Bible behind it.

The top of his head exploded and the body fell.

She was at the tent. She pushed Michael inside. "Get everything of ours together—hurry—throw it in any way you can."

She stuffed her clothes, all the food she had—the spare ammo for her husband's .45, the pistol itself—all of it into her knapsack. The picture—she glanced at it for an instant —her wedding dress—it had burned in the ruins of her house. His tuxedo—it was gone as well. The picture— water stained, dirty, cracked. She shoved it in the knapsack.

"Momma!"

She wheeled, reaching unconsciously for the Trapper .45 on her right hip, thumbing back the hammer, pointing the gun instinctively, the Soviet soldier raising the muzzle of his assault rifle.

She fired—the Soviet soldier's face exploded.

"Ohh, my God," she whispered.

She upped the pistol's safety, stuffing it back in the holster at her hip, then grabbed up her M-16.

She worked the bolt, chambering the top round.

"Grab all the ammo," she shrieked, catching up the knapsack. She reached into her hip pocket, found her other handkerchief and wrapped it around her left hand—the hand burned, was stiff—but she could move the fingers. She gripped the front handguard of the M-16, her right fist on the pistol grip, the knapsack slung across her back.

"Come on, Michael—gotta find your sister—and Millie, too."

She pushed through the tent flap, stepping over the dead Russian soldier. Gunfire from the helicopter above laced the center of the street, running men and women dying.

She pushed Michael ahead of her. "Toward the fence where the children play—hurry!"

Carrying a knapsack and a second sack loaded with ammunition and spare magazines, her son ran ahead of her, Sarah stopping to pump the trigger of the M-16, catching a Soviet soldier in the chest. She started to run again, the whooshing sound—she guessed it was a mortar. The tent behind her exploded, the tents on each side catching fire, someone running from the nearest tent—she couldn't tell if it were a man or a woman, the body a living torch, screams shrieking from inside the flames.

She pumped the trigger of the M-16—a long burst, the body tumbling to the ground, the screaming stopped.

She kept running, Michael ten yards ahead of her, already beside the fence. "Get through and onto the other side—hurry, Michael!"

The boy slipped through the fence, starting to run across the corraled area. She reached the fence, climbing up, rolling, half falling down, firing the M-16 into a knot of Russian soldiers too close to her, gunfire ripping into the fence posts and runners, the M-16 bucking in her hands, two of the Russians going down.

She rammed a fresh magazine into the rifle, stuffing the empty into her jeans waist band. She made to fire—nothing happened.

She worked the bolt, letting it fly forward. Nothing happened again as she fired.

One of the Russians remained. He was wounded, on his feet, running toward her.

She looked down at the rifle as she worked the bolt—the bolt wouldn't pick up the top round, wouldn't chamber it.

"Damn," she shouted.

"Damnit!"

The Russian was less than ten yards from her, his arms raising as he shouldered his assault rifle.

Sarah dropped the rifle, reaching for the Trapper .45, thumbing down the safety, extending the pistol at arms length—she pumped the trigger once, then once again, then once again, the Russian's body stopping as though frozen, the assault rifle dropping from his hands as he lurched forward. She fired the .45—again, then again, the slide locking open, the Russian falling, against the fence runners, his body hanging there, inches from her face.

She pushed the magazine release, taking the empty magazine and pocketing it, then finding the second loaded spare Bill Mulliner had given her. She stuffed it up the butt of the pistol, thumbed down the slide stop.

She picked up the malfunctioning M-16 in her left hand, backing away from the fence, the cocked .45 in her right fist.

"Momma!"

She looked over her shoulder.

Michael—and someone pulling him into the bushes.

She started to run, toward the far side of the corral, to the fence, through the fence this time rather than over it, the .45 extending ahead of her.

"Momma!"

It was Annie's voice this time.

She was ready to kill—but the red-haired head that bobbed from behind the hedgerow—Bill Mulliner.

"Mrs. Rourke—come on!"

She started to run, the whirring of the helicopter rotor blades overhead. Instinctively, she threw herself down, machinegun fire tearing into the ground on both sides of her as she looked up, the underbelly of the green chopper passing over her head, the rotor sound fading.

She pushed herself up, upping the safety on the Trapper .45, running.

"Sarah—over here!" It was Mary Mulliner.

She saw Bill Mulliner now—Michael, Annie and Millie Jenkins with Mary.

"Halt!"

The accented English—hard to understand, but easy to understand as well.

She wheeled, depressing the thumb safety—two Soviet soldiers. She pumped the trigger of the Trapper .45 once, hearing a burst of gunfire from behind her, lighter sounding like an M-16. She threw herself to the dirt, firing her pistol again and again, hearing more of the M-16 fire from behind her, the Russian nearest her firing his AK-47 wildly as he went down, falling, his head slapping against the dirt inches from hers. The second Russian fell—backward, the body bouncing once.

She pushed herself to her feet, turned—Michael and Annie stood beside Bill Mulliner. The red-haired boy knelt on the ground, his mother further back in the trees.

Sarah ran toward them.

"Bill—what—"

She looked over his shoulder. Millie Jenkins—the girl whose father was tortured to death by brigands, whose mother committed suicide after watching it. The girl Sarah had never liked—a quiet girl since the death of her parents. Her skull was split by a bullet, or perhaps more than one.

Bill Mulliner cradled her in his arms.

"Bill—Bill—Bill!"

He looked over his shoulder.

"Ma'am—"

"We've gotta get out of here," and she picked up his M-16, giving hers to Michael. "Don't try using this—something wrong—maybe the clip." Her husband had always told her to call them magazines, she suddenly remembered.

"Bill!"

"But ma'am—gotta bury—"

"Carry her—we'll bury her later—come on—come on—now!"

She pushed Michael and Annie ahead of her, toward the trees where Mary waited. Bill Mulliner was walking—not fast—he held the girl in his arms, blood drenching the front of his clothes.

Sarah Rourke shifted the M-16's muzzle from side to side, running—her lungs ached, her shins ached. There were Russians everywhere—she would run for a long time still, she knew.

# Chapter 59

Cole had remained quiet—stayed to himself. Rourke watched him as they walked, having taken the defile rather than the higher ground. He watched him because he distrusted him. But at least the fight had silenced him.

Natalia moved well, but without the usual spring to her step. Rubenstein still carried her pack, Rourke having taken her rifle. The woman now walked only with the double flap holsters containing the custom Smith L-Frames Sam Chambers had given her—these her only burden.

He watched her now—she seemed cold, the borrowed parka held close around her, the hood up, covering the dark, almost black hair which normally fell past her shoulders. He missed seeing it.

O'Neal walked beside him. "Doctor Rourke—how much longer?"

"We should be able to see Filmore once we get over the rise—then maybe a couple of hours more."

"I don't think the major is gonna make it that long."

Rourke nodded, then added, "Neither do I—once we get out of the defile, we can rest for a while—maybe take a few hours to sleep. She needs it—all of us do."

He glanced at his watch—it would be dark in less than an hour—a good time to rest. He judged them still having ten minutes more walking time in the defile—that would leave plenty of time to set up camp and post sentries.

But as yet, there had been no sign of the wildmen—only the sixth sense that they were out there. This had kept him driving them all throughout the day.

"Think those crazy people know we're here?"

"Yeah," Rourke said through his teeth.

"Think they're gonna attack?"

"Yeah—maybe not for a while yet—if they waited this long—" He stopped—in the fading reddish sun he caught the glint of steel in the rocks. He kept walking. "O'Neal—without having your people change their pace—without anything—tell them to be ready for it—we've got company."

O'Neal started to look up. "Don't—up in those rocks to our left—gonna spring it on us when we reach the end of the defile—maybe just before."

Rourke quickened his pace, but only slightly, leaving O'Neal gradually more and more to his rear, catching up with Natalia and Rubenstein.

"Here," he rasped through his teeth, Natalia turning to look at him, her eyes wide, staring, "Carry your rifle—gonna need it."

Paul glanced toward him, never changing his pace. "Up in the rocks? I saw something catch the sun."

"Rifle maybe—I figure they're up there."

"Wonderful," Rubenstein groaned.

"John—if you have to—I'll slow you—"

"Shut up," he smiled, walking past her then as she took her M-16.

Cole and one of his troopers led the ragged column. Rourke—slowly—caught up with him.

"Cole—up in the rocks—got company. Don't act differently—just keep walking."

"Aww, shit—if we hadn't brought the woman we woulda been outa here by now—"

"Shut up and listen. These guys weren't following us—probably got Filmore Air Force base ringed—that's a good sign—must mean somebody's alive in there. We just cut in on the wildmen—they weren't following us."

"I feel like I'm playin' cowboys and Indians—"

"Yeah, well—good similarity, I guess. When the shooting starts, you and your private there—take up positions on each side of the defile and start pumping up into the rocks—I'll take the others through, then Rubenstein and I will set up covering fire from the other side of the defile for you and your man to get through—then we try for Filmore as fast as we can."

"What're ya gonna do about the woman—"

"Carry her if I have to—she's my responsibility. You just do what you've gotta do and it'll work out."

Rourke slowed his pace, risking a glance up into the rocks—he saw movement, but indefinite movement—he wasn't certain.

The reflection could have been from a natural cause—a hiker could have left a bottle up in the rocks ten years earlier, rain washing it clean enough to catch the sun.

But he didn't think so—instinct again.

He looked ahead as he slowed enough for Natalia and Paul to catch up with him.

The defile narrowed into a wide "V" shape as they reached the height of the rise—if he were setting an ambush, it would be there. There was no way to get out of the defile except through the V-notch.

"John—"

He glanced to his left, Natalia beside him. "What is it?"

"I feel them—up there, waiting."

"Yeah—me, too," Rubenstein said, at his right.

"When it comes—Paul—you get Natalia through—"

"I can take care of myself—"

"Paul—you do what I say—then set up on the other side of the defile. As soon as I get through with O'Neal and his men. Natalia—you stick with O'Neal—Paul and I'll be covering—"

A gunshot, a heavy caliber—a hunting weapon rather than an assault rifle—echoed across the defile. A scream—

O'Neal was shouting, "They got one of my men!"

Rourke flicked the safety off the CAR-15, pulling out the buttstock, bringing the rifle to his shoulder, the scope covers already gone. "Run for it," he shouted, firing up into the rocks.

"Come on, Natalia!" Rubenstein shouted. Rourke didn't look. He spotted something move in the rocks, laying the Colt three power scope on it, tripping the trigger.

A man's shape threw itself up beyond the scope's reticle, then flipped over the edge of the rocks. Rourke shifted the scope, searching for another target, gunfire from around him hammering up into the rocks, the powdering of granite evident everywhere as he searched for a target. He found one—a man with a scoped bolt action rifle—perhaps the sniper who'd killed one of O'Neal's men. Rourke opened fire, a two round semi-automatic burst, the body twitching once, then once again, the rifle falling into airspace, the body tumbling after it.

Rourke brought his rifle down, starting to run, Paul and Natalia already ahead of him, running, but slowly, nearing the defile's V-notch, Cole and his private already in the notch, firing up into the rocks, O'Neal's men running toward the notch as well.

"Keep 'em moving, lieutenant!"

O'Neal shouted something Rourke couldn't hear, automatic weapons fire coming down on them from the rocks. Rourke was nearing the V-notch now, rock faces on both sides of him, bullets impacting there, ricocheting, whining, rock chips pelting at him, the dust from the rocks thick as automatic weapons fire hammered into the rock walls.

Rourke dropped behind a fallen rock—a boulder-sized chunk of granite, jagged at the top, the CAR-15 coming up to his shoulder. He snapped off three shots toward the rocks, not having clear targets in view, gunfire hammering into the boulder.

He pushed up, acquiring a target in the scope, firing, shifting the scope as the body started to fall from the rocks.

He fired again, missing, gunfire coming back at him. He ducked down, a long burst hammering into the boulder above his head and the rock wall. He pushed up, finding his target with the scope, working the CAR-15's trigger in and out and in and out—two shots, then another two shots, then another, the figure in the rocks spinning, falling back, out of sight.

Rourke got to his feet, O'Neal and the others past him now, Cole and his private hunkered down in the V-notch, firing up into the rocks. Rourke ran past them, throwing himself through, rolling, the rocks on both sides seeming to explode with ricochets and dust.

"John—over here!"

Rourke saw him—Rubenstein. Rourke pushed to his feet, half ran, half threw himself toward the protection of three massive boulders, dragging himself behind them.

Rubenstein had Natalia's M-16, firing up into the rocks.

Rourke snatched a fresh magazine for the CAR-15 from his musette bag, dumping the partially spent one, ramming it into his belt. He whacked the base of the magazine, seating it, then threw the rifle to his shoulder, firing up into the rocks at the wildmen. One man in his scope—one man dead. He shifted the scope. A woman, or a tall, long-haired man who seemed very thin. Rourke fired, the body falling from sight.

"Cole—you and your man!" Rourke shouted over the gunfire.

The fire from Rubenstein's M-16 increased, Rourke feeling the hot brass pelting at him, feeling it against his neck, feeling one of the empties sliding down his shirt front.

He kept firing. Another wildman under his scope—he shot the man twice, the body tumbling from the rocks, a scream echoing across the defile.

"Here we come," Cole shouted, Rourke glancing away from his scope, seeing Cole and the Army private running. Rourke looked back to the scope, finding another target, firing, firing again, the target going down.

"They're through—come on, John," Rubenstein shouted.

"Get going," Rourke rasped, glancing to his left as Paul was up and running, firing a burst half over his shoulder into the rocks.

Rourke dropped the partially shot out magazine, stuffing it into his belt, inserting a fresh thirty up the well. He started to run, turning every few steps, pumping shots up into the rocks. Beyond the V-notch there had been a rocky trail, narrow. He ran along it now, firing out the magazine in the CAR-15, the trail taking a sharp bend to his right and down, gunfire hammering into the rock wall to his right as he took the bend.

He stopped, the ricocheting sounds of bullets hitting granite stopping—he was out of range.

He looked ahead of him.

A valley.

Natalia sat on her haunches, Paul stooped over beside her, her face pale, her head between her knees. O'Neal's left arm was streaming blood, but he stood erect. One of O'Neal's men lay on the ground, the front of his peacoat stained and wet with blood.

In the valley beyond the trail and stretching below them—Rourke walked forward, toward the edge of the trail—he could see the outline of a fenced military enclosure—Filmore Air Force Base. There were small craters in the far side of the valley—to the north. Nothing grew in the valley—brown trees, brown grass—he couldn't hear a bird chirp.

"Radiation seems okay—what the hell happened?" Rubenstein asked, suddenly beside him.

Rourke looked at the younger man. "Neutron bombs—the craters are from the impact areas."

"John—" Natalia, pale, closing her eyes as she spoke, turned her face up toward the sky, her voice odd sounding. "Why did they stop shooting—why aren't they—"

"Following?" He interrupted. "Everything that was here is dead—maybe some personnel at the base—but they're afraid of radiation." He looked away from her—it would have been green before the Night of The War. Now it was brown and dead.

There were wounds to treat—the man on the ground seemed the most serious. "Natalia—when you can, take care of O'Neal's bleeding."

Rourke started toward the missile technician on the ground—like O'Neal, his missiles fired, he was out of a job. Rourke bent to check his pulse—he was out of life as well.

If the warheads still existed, to get them out past the wildmen would be nearly impossible, Rourke realized.

And there was still Cole.

He thumbed closed the eyelids of the dead man, stood up and removed his sunglasses.

"We can rest here for a little while—move out into the valley in a few hours—Paul and I'll take the geiger counters and run point for radiation."

He found another injured man, mechanically starting to treat him—it was minor.

He wondered who cared for his wife and two children—were they alive? He closed his eyes and told himself they were, and that he would find them, then opened his eyes and inspected the injured man's wound. "Paul—get my medical kit—got a bullet to take out here."